SUNSET CHARADE

SUNSET
Charade

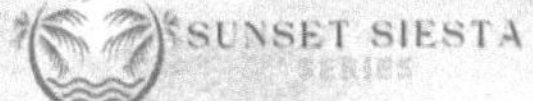

SUNSET CHARADE

A Sunset Siesta Novella

Sunset Siesta Series

ERIN BROCKUS

GREEN SAGE
PRESS

Print ISBN: 978-1-957003-47-4

Chapter One

BRYNN

I ALWAYS IMAGINED my next big life change would start with a cosmic sign—maybe a flamingo holding a banner reading *This Way, Brynn!* Instead, my welcome was a cheerful carved board hanging from a crossbeam, its painted *Welcome to Sunset Siesta Resort* faded by years of salt and sun.

My suitcase wheels rattled along the shell-strewn path, past a two-story room block whose faded pastel paint and sagging rooflines felt as tired as I did after my flight from Atlanta. The salt-laced air of the Florida Keys, however, was a time machine, transporting me straight back to the summer I turned seventeen. I stopped and gripped my long brown hair in one hand, the breeze stirring up old memories—long beach days with Holly, the giggly hush of post-midnight adventures, a first beer that had tasted more of regret than anything else.

But I wasn't here for a trip down memory lane. I was

here with two jobs: survive my cousin Holly Shaw's destination wedding without becoming a human exhibit for family pity, and, more secretly, figure out if I had the guts to give my *what if* life a fighting chance.

The lobby's air conditioning hit me like a slap. The decor attempted to capture Old Florida, with bamboo furniture, faded manatee prints, and a taxidermied marlin mounted like a sentinel above the reception desk.

A woman in a pineapple-print blouse and a nametag reading *Dana* smiled. "Checking in?"

"Brynn Vance," I replied.

She typed, her nails clicking crisply, before sliding a key folder across the counter. "Ah, you're part of the wedding party! Room 215. The welcome mixer is at the Tidal Hops brewpub tonight at six."

"Great. Anything I should know about the room?"

Dana shrugged. "It's pretty standard. I doubt much has changed since your last visit. Don't feed the iguanas."

Laughing, I saluted her with the key folder and stepped back into the breezy air. The walk to my room was a nostalgia bomb. Winding shell paths crunched under my suitcase, and the sea breeze whipped my hair into the same hopeless knots I remembered. Back then, this place was the backdrop for Holly's wild schemes. Now, she was getting married while I was here solo, which felt both poetic and tragic.

My second-floor room overlooked the ocean, its paint faded from aqua to the color of hospital scrubs, but the deck was freshly swept. I flopped onto the clean, palm-print comforter, my spine realigning. If this was my *find yourself* journey, the bar was set at shabby chic. I could work with that.

I unpacked a wardrobe of compromises, choosing a blue linen dress that had survived years of first-grade classroom drama and a pair of sandals I'd bought just for the trip. I arranged my toiletries with the efficiency of a woman trying to impose order on her own chaos. On the desk, my welcome folder held a map, an itinerary, and a handwritten note from Holly.

BRYNN!

You made it! Don't let my mom rope you into any "fun runs." Meet you at the taproom at six for pre-game drinks. We're going to make so many bad decisions. (Kidding. Mostly.)

Love you more than SPF 50,
Holly

I SMILED. Only Holly could make a wedding sound like an illicit adventure.

Sliding open the door to the deck revealed a sliver of sandy beach that arched toward a weathered wooden pier, the water glittering as the sun began its lazy descent. Two pelicans argued on a mooring post.

This is it. My second chance.

I closed my eyes, the warm air filling my lungs. If I stood still enough, I could almost picture seventeen-year-old me still on the sand, plotting how to outrun the future.

The future arrived as another text from Holly.

Holly: The resort is still so unique. Rustic
charm with a laid-back vibe. Not fancy, but
it has character! Tidal Hops is great. Hurry!

I RECHECKED MY HAIR, hesitating. I was used to minimizing myself—shrink to fit, blend in, don't ruffle feathers. Walking into a room of strangers and family set my stomach tap-dancing.

But tonight was for Holly. And maybe for the Brynn who wondered what it felt like to own the room.

I slipped on my sandals and stepped into the humid, golden evening. The path to the taproom curved along the water, lit by somewhat rusty solar lights. I skirted a cluster of guests already deep into the welcome punch and ducked into the ladies' room for a pep talk.

"Don't look like you're casing the joint," I muttered to the mirror. "Just be normal."

My reflection looked unconvinced, but I squared my shoulders anyway and went to face the mixer.

Tidal Hops had cheery turquoise walls hung with vintage wooden surfboards and a ceiling strung with LED string lights. Wooden beams were etched with initials, and the walls held framed photos of fish and locals with fish. Every table was packed, the noise level just shy of a rock concert, and the air thick with the smell of hoppy beer and fried seafood.

I barely made it past the hostess stand before a blur of floral print collided with me. Holly, bride-to-be and my lifelong partner in chaos, grinned after swallowing a mouthful of shrimp cocktail.

"Brynn! You made it!" she shrieked, shoving a skewer of something unidentifiable into my hand.

I chewed, hoping for the best. "Is this… calamari?"

Holly shrugged. "I think so. Josh's family is super into 'authentic coastal cuisine.'" She used air quotes and eyed my outfit. "You look amazing! Is that the Atlanta breakup dress?"

I coughed. "My *moving on with my life* dress, but yes."

Holly leaned in. "Good woman! Try the Tidal Hops IPA. It's pretty damn good. I've had two glasses."

"Never would have guessed. Where's the clan?"

She nodded toward the bar. "Mom's making the rounds. Josh is getting a hops tutorial from the owner. Uh-oh. Here comes trouble."

The warning came too late. Aunt Carol, her brown-gray hair helmeted against the humidity, advanced with a man my age in a blue polo, trailing her like a remora. My soul tried to leave my body.

"Oh, look at that!" Holly chirped, already scurrying away. "So many bride things to do. See you later!"

"Brynn, darling!" Aunt Carol sing-songed, seizing my elbow with the triumphant air of a dog show handler. "Todd, this is my niece. You remember Todd, don't you, Brynn? My neighbor's son?"

It wasn't hard to recognize Todd. He was my age—twenty-nine—but he never changed. Average height, average build, average everything. He'd worked at a big-box electronics store for years.

"Hey, Brynn." His handshake was wet and limp. "Wow, you look exactly like your Facebook picture."

"Thanks, I guess?" I tried to pull my hand back, but he held on.

"Todd was just saying how he's always wanted to see the Keys," Aunt Carol continued conspiratorially. "And it's so much more fun with someone who knows her way around. So I convinced him to tag along with me!"

"Dove Key is fascinating." Todd launched into a rapid-fire monologue about it, a firehose of unsolicited facts. Then he jerked a thumb at the speakers pumping out Jimmy Buffett and sounding wonderful. "The midrange is totally blunted. If they upgraded the mixer, the whole vibe would change."

"Oh, okay." I had no idea how to respond to that. He couldn't be trying to flirt, could he?

Aunt Carol beamed as if he'd just solved world hunger. "Isn't he smart?"

"By the way, I'm in Room 217, right next to yours," Todd added. "I brought my Fire Stick—I can reprogram it for premium channels and install a Wi-Fi range extender for you. The repeaters are on the wrong side for your room's western exposure."

Jeeezus.

He smiled, oblivious, and handed me a business card with a QR code. "I made these for networking, but they're multipurpose. I'll be your date for the weekend. If you get bored, just knock."

It was the saddest thing I'd ever been handed.

"I don't want to hover, so you kids have fun," Aunt Carol said, squeezing my shoulder. "Brynn, dear, don't let Todd hog the karaoke mic this time!"

Red flamed across Todd's face. "I got banned from the last holiday party for doing 'Bohemian Rhapsody' in its entirety. That song must be respected."

I made a noise that was half laugh, half choke. "Excuse me. I need a refill."

I fled to the bar, my hands shaking so badly it took me three tries to get the bartender's attention. He had an easy grin and light-brown hair escaping from under a Tidal Hops baseball cap. "You look like you need a drink. What can I get for you?"

"Whatever tropical IPA you have," I managed.

He slid a frosty glass across the bar. "Our Sunset Ale. My personal favorite."

I clung to the cold glass, letting it leech the panic from my bloodstream, and took a long, desperate gulp. The beer was crisp and citrusy, with a perfect bitter kick at the end. "Damn. That's really good."

The bartender's grin widened. "Thanks. I'm Braden Coleridge, by the way. The brewmaster."

Before I could reply, a passing server leaned in with an affectionate eye-roll. "He's also the owner. Don't let him fool you."

Braden just shrugged, unbothered, and turned to take another order.

I leaned against the bar, nursing my drink. Of all the futures I'd dreaded, none involved being chaperoned by Todd I-Brought-My-Own-Fire-Stick Peterson. I'd spent months bracing for this trip, worried I'd crumble under family scrutiny. I hadn't considered being courted by a man whose romantic overtures involved optimizing cable packages.

I had no idea what to do next, but water had always soothed me, so I took my beer and slipped out to the waterfront deck. The sunset painted the beach in vivid pink and orange, but I barely noticed, leaning over the railing to let the briny breeze clear my head. I nursed my beer, watching a heron pick its way along the dock pilings. How was I going to survive this weekend?

The universe, a notorious showoff, struck again when Todd materialized beside me. He pointed to the TV over the bar. "Do you like documentaries about shipwrecks?"

I lied. "Not really."

"Oh. Well, maybe we'll find something else to watch."

He stood there, expectant, as if the only barrier between us and true love was a Netflix title.

"Sounds good," I said, my pulse ratcheting up.

"I just thought, if you want to borrow my Fire Stick—"

"That's sweet, Todd," I interrupted, my eyes darting inside as I desperately searched for a lifeline.

My gaze landed on a tall, dark-haired man in a steel-blue button-down being mauled by a cackling redhead. Dean Mercer, the best man. We'd met several times in Atlanta, and he had a face that stuck with you—square jaw, sharp dimple, eyes like glacier runoff. Yeah, that color blue. I'd always pegged him as too handsome, too slick and successful. But the raw, trapped look on his face was so relatable I almost laughed.

Our eyes met.

His eyebrow shot up, the corner of his mouth curling in a silent, *Can you believe this?*

My own lips twitched, and I lifted my glass in salute. His smile widened.

"I should go see if Holly needs help," I told Todd, already moving.

"Totally. See you inside?"

I threaded through the noisy crowd, heart thrumming with reckless energy. Dean had wedged a stool between himself and the relentless redhead, but she just leaned over him, invading his space. I steeled myself, glided up to his open side, and perched on the empty stool.

"There you are," I said with a breathless laugh, wrapping my arm around his broad shoulders. "I've been looking everywhere."

Dean's eyes widened, but he thought fast. He pivoted, his knee bumping mine.

"Baby," he drawled with deadpan affection that almost made me choke. "You're late."

"Don't start," I improvised, leaning in. "You know I get lost in these places."

The redhead blinked. "Sorry, I didn't realize—"

"It's fine," I cut her off with a paint-stripping smile. "I'm used to the effect he has on women. But I'm afraid he's taken." I patted his shoulder, and he slid his hand over mine in a perfect fit. She wilted and vanished.

We exhaled in synchronized relief.

"Thanks, Brynn." Dean's voice was low and warm. "God, thank you. I owe you my potential first kid."

"Only if he comes with a range extender and a Fire Stick," I deadpanned, then waved absently when Dean's brow scrunched up. "Long story."

He grinned, signaling the bartender. "So. Fake boyfriend or plausible deniability?"

"A little of both. I'm being hunted by the wedding's official sad-single-girl wrangler."

His face lit up with understanding. "Aunt Carol?"

"She never misses."

"Mine is the mother of the groom. She thinks I'm a flight risk. We could help each other out." The proposal hung between us, a current of pure possibility. "We pretend to be together, everyone leaves us alone, and we drink in peace."

"Tempting. But are you any good at the *together* part?"

A slow, lazy smile spread across his face. "I'm an excellent fake boyfriend. Rave reviews."

I laughed. "Fine. But if you ditch me, I reserve the right to set fire to your luggage."

"Deal," he leaned in, eyes dancing. "Good thing I travel light."

As I sipped my beer, I took in Dean's face up close— faint five o'clock shadow, a tiny scar above his eyebrow, a mouth that looked like it could ruin a woman with a single smirk. Tall, dark, and handsome in the flesh. He was trouble, and apparently exactly what I needed.

"So how do we play this?" I asked. "Subtle, or should I start calling you darling?"

Dean's gaze held mine. "Let's go big. They'll expect subtle."

He stood and offered his hand. I took it, my palm fitting perfectly against his as he led me through the bar, turning heads. The heat of his body radiated through his linen shirt. This was supposed to be an act, but the chemistry was disorienting and real.

At the edge of the deck, he stopped, his breath stirring the hair at my temple.

"You're shaking," he said quietly.

"It's the IPA," I lied. "Hoppy."

He smiled, tightening his grip on my waist. "Just checking. I don't want my girlfriend fainting on day one."

"Brynn! There you are!" Aunt Carol marched up, towing a crestfallen Todd.

Dean straightened, murmuring, "Showtime."

"Brynn, dear, you left so suddenly," Aunt Carol said. "Everything all right?"

"Never better." A surge of wicked delight ran through me. "Dean was just about to show me the pier."

He played his part perfectly, pulling me snug against him. "We were getting some air."

Todd's face fell as his gaze dropped to Dean's hand on my waist. "Oh. I didn't realize you two were—"

"Together? It's pretty new," I said, turning my face up to Dean's, marveling at how easily the lie came.

He didn't hesitate, cupping my cheek. "Yeah. She's the best thing to happen to me in a long time."

The cheesy words landed deep in my chest. I leaned into his touch, then handed Todd his business card back.

"Sorry, Todd. I wasn't sure if you were just being friendly, so I didn't say anything."

"Well," Aunt Carol sniffed. "Isn't that something. Todd, didn't you want to check the sound system inside?"

Todd blinked. "Yeah. I'll just, uh, be over there."

He shuffled away, business card clutched in his hand like a tragic souvenir. After a curious look at us, Aunt Carol followed.

Dean waited until they were gone before dropping his arm. "Too much?"

"No, it was perfect," I said, feeling dizzy. "You even convinced me."

He ducked his head. "Sorry. I have a tendency to go overboard."

"At least you commit," I said, steadying myself with my cold glass. "More than I can say for most men I've known."

"Don't compliment me yet. You might be disappointed." He leaned on the railing beside me. "Are you here just to support Holly? It can't be just to dodge Todd."

The truth slipped out before I could stop it. "My ex told me I was *utterly unambitious*. He said I'd never take a real risk." My voice was sour with the memory. "So I saw you across the bar and took one."

Dean nodded. "People say crap like that because they're scared you'll do something they never could. Trust me." he added softly, "I know the type."

A comfortable silence settled between us as I wondered if we had more in common than I'd thought.

"I'm not usually this reckless," I admitted.

He smiled, his eyes crinkling. "Good. You'll need your wits to survive this weekend." His fingertips skated over my knuckles, and this time, it didn't feel like an act at all.

Across the room, Holly caught my eye and lifted her glass in a salute. For the first time since arriving, I felt something other than dread. I felt hope. And a little bit of fire.

Dean's gaze was steady. "Ready to make them all jealous?"

"Absolutely." I let him pull me into the crowd, two halves of a perfect, improbable lie. For now, I was exactly where I wanted to be.

Chapter Two

DEAN

THE ONLY WAY TO survive a destination wedding is with a clear exit strategy. My job was to protect multi-million-dollar portfolios from emotional, irrational impulses. Yet here I was, staring at the sun-bleached ceiling of a hotel room, my strategy in tatters after one night. Beyond the curtains, the ocean cast rippling patterns across the wall, filling the room with the kind of light that made hungover people reconsider their life decisions. I wasn't hungover, but I was in the early throes of regret.

Last night, fake dating Brynn Vance had seemed like a logical, heaven-sent play. But it was already becoming a problem. I'd spent the last ten minutes replaying the look on her face last night—that shaky moment when I'd pulled her close. The flush on her cheeks, and the quick dart of her hazel eyes to mine. I'd casually known her for years, so why hadn't I ever noticed the extraordinary gold and green flecks in her irises? This was supposed to be an act, but somewhere between the staged possessiveness and her body pressed against mine, it had started to feel damn good.

That was the problem with Brynn. On paper, she was everything I avoided—soft edges, big heart, the kind of person who probably owned a crockpot. In reality, she had a sharp, unfiltered sincerity I didn't know how to handle. She was so transparently good it bordered on reckless. Most people like her annoyed the hell out of me. But the Brynn of last night had been the opposite of irritating.

I dragged myself out of bed. The room was straight out of a 1980s travel brochure—shell-shaped pillows, prints of beachscapes. From the balcony, Dove Key was a parade of pastel buildings and palm trees. Sunset Siesta Resort was working the Old Florida charm so hard it felt like it might collapse under its own marketing. But I had to admit it all worked for them. I made my way to the in-room coffee station. The coffee was terrible. Wincing, I added extra cream.

My wish for the day was to avoid anything resembling a wedding event. But that was a futile wish. I was here for Josh Bennett. We'd been best friends since college, and if he wanted to end his life as a free-thinking, single man, I'd do my best to support that decision. Even if I couldn't disagree more.

A brisk knock came at the door—the authoritative thud of someone who had no qualms about waking the dead. I sighed and crossed the room before opening the door to a woman around my age with brown hair trying to escape its ponytail. A clipboard was tucked under one arm like an extension of her spine. She offered a bright, efficient smile.

"Mr. Mercer? Dean Mercer?"

"That's me."

She extended her hand, and we exchanged a firm shake. "Harper Coleridge, general manager. Sorry to drop in, but we like to ensure our VIP guests have everything they need." I ushered her into the room, where she did a quick visual sweep and handed me a heavy white envelope. "You somehow didn't get a welcome packet yesterday."

Stifling another sigh, I accepted the folder. "Thanks. I'm all set on activities."

She arched a brow, and the smile returned. "I noticed you and Ms. Vance at the welcome mixer. Best man and maid of honor are a couple too. I love it!"

I smirked. "Wasn't aware we made that much of an impression."

"Well, it's my job to notice things like that. I wanted to make sure you knew about the couple's retreat package. You'll find the details in the envelope."

I opened it. Glossy brochures, coupons, and a detailed itinerary. "Couple's paddleboard yoga?" I read aloud. "You're kidding."

"Not at all. We're proud of our holistic programming. We also include a sunset sail, a tandem kayak excursion, and a cooking class. Of course, none of it is mandatory, but folks really enjoy the variety." Harper's tone was professional, but a glint of mischief lit her eyes, as if she could read my mind.

I narrowed my eyes at her. "Sounds like emotional blackmail."

She laughed, the managerial mask slipping. "Different strokes for different folks, then." She paused at the threshold. "Oh. My brother Eli runs the dive shop. Just want to remind you about your dive trip at nine. Ms. Vance will be there too, of course."

I nodded. "I'll be there. Too bad Josh and Holly bailed on the underwater adventure."

Harper tucked the clipboard under her arm. "They were disappointed too. Last-minute wedding attire fitting. This was the only time the seamstress and tailor had free." With that, she was gone, leaving the faint scent of coconut sunscreen and absolute authority.

I stared at the itinerary. No way was I attempting paddleboard yoga or a damn cooking class. But my eye snagged on the wedding party dive. The dive that was now just Brynn and me. The fake dating scheme had gone from a clever ruse to a full-blown performance, with props and an audience ready to pounce. I drained my coffee with a grimace and braced myself for the show.

The air on the resort pier was thick with salt and the whine of a fishing charter. Brynn perched on a bench at the end of the dock, her hair in a neat ponytail. She wore a fitted rash guard over athletic swim shorts, an outfit both modest and sexy. She scanned the beach, her face open and unguarded, as if she were genuinely happy to be here. I didn't trust it.

"Nice of you to make it," she called as I approached. "I was starting to think you bailed too."

I held up the activity vouchers. "Turns out skipping town isn't on the itinerary. Only the bride and groom had permission slips. Ready?"

She shot me a smile. "Only if you promise not to drown. I'll never live it down."

I liked her wry wit. "I was hoping to fake an injury and spend the weekend at the poolside bar. Do they serve real drinks here, or just weird blue things with umbrellas?"

She squinted, amusement in her gold-brown eyes. "Are you really this allergic to fun, or is it an elaborate hoax?"

"Fun is fine in moderation. I just don't like it forced down my throat."

A shadow loomed behind her. "Ladies and gentlemen, welcome to the only adventure in town worth missing brunch for."

The man was over six feet of laid-back bravado, sandy blond hair sticking up like he'd just surfed. He wore a Sunset Siesta T-shirt with *Dive Staff* on the sleeve and board shorts, his skin tanned a deep caramel.

"Brynn, you never warned me your boyfriend was so uptight," he said, grinning as he performed an elaborate handshake she already knew.

"Eli, meet Dean," Brynn said. "Dean, Eli Coleridge. Dive instructor and Dove Key's answer to a walking liability waiver."

Eli laughed and clapped me on the back hard enough to realign my spine. "Nice. Fresh meat. So the big certification dive is finally over, huh? You ready to join the cool-kids club?"

"As ready as I'll ever be," I said. The days of intensive pool sessions and book work, then diving in a quarry to get certified, had been a blur. I'd passed the tests, but my confidence was purely theoretical. "Let's do this."

Eli grinned. "Hardcore. You'll fit right in." He eyed the activity voucher in my pocket. "Aw, the couple's package. My personal favorite."

Brynn gave me a sidelong look as she looped her arm through mine. "We thought it would be a bonding experience."

Eli made a face of exaggerated disgust. "You two are gross. I love it. Let's get you fitted."

He led us into the gear shack, an oversized shed that smelled of neoprene and seawater. He handed me a wetsuit and fins. "The usual gear, hotshot. Try not to rip it. Stuff's expensive."

I couldn't help grinning back.

Brynn slipped into her suit with the practiced ease of someone who had done this dozens of times. My own movements were still clumsy, calculated. I double-checked every strap and seal, the instructor's voice a mantra in my head: *Complacency kills*.

"Relax, Mercer," she said, her voice low. "You're a certified diver, remember? I'm sure you aced the pool drills."

"The ocean has more things that can eat you," I muttered.

"Maybe a few." She grinned. "We should probably coordinate our story before we're surrounded by nosy guests again. You want to take the lead?"

"Let's go with: met at a bar, got drunk, made a terrible decision. It's closest to the truth."

She shook her head. "You have the romantic instincts of a wet sandbag."

"Thank you. I work hard at it."

"Okay, question," she said as we walked toward the boat. "When did you know you were in love with me?"

I rolled my eyes. "We're really doing this?"

"Eli will ask. So will everyone else. Practice."

I feigned concentration. "I'll say it was the time you beat me at trivia night and did a victory dance on the bar."

She snorted. "That never happened."

"Exactly. I'm establishing you as a liar and a show-off. Takes the pressure off me."

Brynn nudged me with her shoulder, her smile more natural for a second. "Fine. But for the record, I would absolutely win at trivia. And I'd do the dance."

Eli beckoned us over. "Lovebirds! Pre-dive briefing."

He ran through the plan for the site—depth, expected currents, types of animals, points of interest. He looked directly at me, the smartass persona falling away. "Dean, this is your first open-water dive since your checkout. We stick together. Brynn's your buddy, but I'm the boss. Any problems, you signal me first. Got it?"

"Got it," I said, appreciating his professionalism.

"Brynn's an old pro," Eli continued, testing the tanks with a sharp hiss. "But everyone does a buddy check, every time."

We followed him onto the dive boat. *Sunset Diver* was a sleek fiberglass boat with plenty of room. We were lucky to have it to ourselves. I sat next to Brynn behind Eli, the engine's rumble vibrating through the hull as I went through my own mental checklist.

As he guided the boat away from the pier, he glanced over his shoulder at Brynn. "So when was the last time you were down here, anyway? Feels like it's been a while."

"It has," she said, her voice a little wistful. "Probably three or four years ago, for that disastrous family reunion my mom planned."

I turned to her, surprised. "You come here often?"

She laughed, a sound clear and natural over the hum of the motor. "Not exactly a regular, but Holly and I used to spend a week here almost every summer when we were kids. And teenagers. This place is practically a second home."

That explained it—the easy way she navigated the grounds, her familiarity with the staff.

"You still teaching kiddos up in Atlanta?" Eli asked, his eyes on the channel markers.

"Yep, still wrangling six-year-olds," she confirmed. "Though I've been getting an itch for a change lately."

Eli shrugged casually. "Well, if you ever get serious

about it, I imagine you could get a job at the elementary school here. It survived all six of us Coleridge kids, so it's probably a pretty safe place to work." He grinned. "Built like a bunker."

Brynn's gaze drifted to the mangrove-lined shore, a thoughtful expression settling on her face. She was quiet for a moment. "Teach in Dove Key… It sounds wonderful, idyllic even." Then her expression clouded slightly. "But my job in Atlanta is good too. I love working with my kids. I guess I'd worry a teaching job here would be the same life, just transplanted to a different town. I'm not sure that's the change I'm looking for, you know."

She laughed self-consciously, the moment passing, but her words lingered. That flicker of deep-seated restlessness in her eyes was impossible to ignore. It was a look I recognized from my own reflection.

The boat slowed over the dive site. Twenty feet down, the reef was a garden of color and motion. Eli moored us to the ball floating on the surface. "All right, folks. Gear up. Buddy checks."

Brynn turned to me, her expression shifting from carefree to focused. She went through the checks methodically, her hands moving over my gear with a competence that was both reassuring and attractive. When it was my turn, I did the same, my fumbling overshadowed by muscle memory. As I checked her tank valve, I caught her glancing at me, not with a teacher's evaluative squint, but with something softer, like she was genuinely looking forward to sharing this.

Maybe I was too.

Then Eli shouted, "Let's dive!" and I remembered I was about to hurl myself into the ocean. The anticipation ratcheted up, a mix of caution and thrill.

Jumping off the stern platform of the boat, the world

above became sealed away behind a wall of blue. My heartbeat was a distant thump compared to the rush of bubbles and the mechanical whir of my breathing. Brynn dropped in after me. We gave each other the okay sign, then began a slow, controlled descent, following Eli through thirty feet of turquoise.

They say the world sounds different underwater. They're not wrong. My movements were cautious, deliberate—a contrast to Brynn, who moved like she belonged here, controlled but loose, letting the water carry her. Being underwater seemed to strip away whatever held her back on land.

At the bottom, the reef stretched in every direction, a vibrant landscape. Fields of soft corals in shades of purple and orange swayed in the gentle current, and delicate sea fans filtered the dappled sunlight. Schools of electric-blue parrotfish and striped sergeant majors darted in and out of the coral heads. My pulse finally leveled, the cautious anxiety giving way to a sense of awe. All my fumbling and focus on the mechanics melted away.

This was what it was all about.

I was so lost in the spectacle that I almost missed Brynn's frantic tapping on my arm. I turned, and she was pointing out into the deep blue, away from the reef, her eyes wide with excitement behind her mask. At first, I saw nothing but hazy, endless water.

Then, a sleek, gray shape materialized from the blue, then another, and another. A pod of six dolphins, gliding past with an effortless grace that made my own deliberate movements feel clumsy and loud. They were silent and majestic, moving as one organism. Two of them broke from the pod, their curiosity evidently getting the better of them. They circled us once, their intelligent eyes taking us in, before peeling off to rejoin their family and disappearing back into the deep. The entire encounter lasted maybe a minute or two, but it felt like a lifetime.

I glanced at Brynn. Her reaction was not the detached cool of an experienced diver. It was absolute joy. Her eyes were crinkling at the corners in a clear smile behind her mask, and she gave a little, ecstatic wiggle that sent a cloud of bubbles toward the surface. She was completely lost in the moment. Not curating it for a story later but living it. It was the same easy happiness I'd seen on the boat, but amplified by the silent, intimate world we were sharing. Then I remembered the game we were supposed to be playing.

We're a couple.

The thought was a sudden, jarring reminder of my role. I reached out and, a little awkwardly, took her hand. She startled for a moment, her head snapping toward me, her eyes questioning. Then she caught on. A slow smile spread across her face, and her fingers laced through mine, a warm, firm pressure in the water. The smooth feel of her hand in mine in this breathtaking world, sent a jolt through me. I liked it. A lot more than I should have.

She gave my hand a little squeeze, then turned to point out a huge parrotfish chomping on a piece of coral. We swam on like that, hand in hand, two halves of a perfect lie.

Then, as we rounded a curve in the reef, Brynn froze. Her hand shot to her mask. A froth of bubbles erupted from her regulator, and she jerked backward, eyes wide.

She was choking.

The sight was so unexpected it short-circuited my own novice nerves. All my self-consciousness vanished, replaced by a singular, clear thought.

Help her.

She was already clawing at her regulator. I moved

toward her, slow and deliberate, just as I'd practiced. I caught her wrist gently. Her frantic eyes locked on mine. I moved my hands in the universal *slow down, breathe* signal.

She hesitated, then nodded. She exhaled, then slowly inhaled but sputtered again. More bubbles, more panic.

I squeezed her hand—*steady*.

I mimed it again, slower. This time she got it, and her breathing began to steady. She blinked at me, gratitude and embarrassment warring behind the glass. We floated, and for once, I was stripped of my bullshit.

A moment later, Eli was there. He gave me a sharp, approving nod, then took over. He got Brynn's attention, gave the *okay* signal, and when she returned a shaky affirmative, he signaled for us to begin a slow, controlled ascent to the safety stop. Grateful to have him managing the situation, I fell in line. My own adrenaline faded as I watched him expertly guide her upward.

On the boat ride back, Brynn was quiet. She sat on the edge of the deck, wringing water from her ponytail as she stared at the horizon.

I tossed her a towel. "You good?"

She nodded but didn't meet my eye. "Fine. I've done a hundred dives and never choked like that."

I sat close enough that our thighs touched. "It happens. But thank you for not dying on my first real dive. Bad for morale."

That got a smile. "Thanks for not making it worse."

I nudged her shoulder. "Thanks for not dragging me to the bottom in your death throes."

She studied me closely, and for a beat, I thought she might say something honest and uncomfortable. Instead, she wrapped the towel around her shoulders. "You hate it here, don't you?"

I blinked. "Excuse me?"

"Dove Key. The water, the people. You spend half your time mocking it and the other half plotting escape."

It stung. "Is this where you tell me to stop being a jerk and appreciate the magic of island life?"

"No. I just wonder what you're so afraid of."

That caught me off guard. "I'm not afraid."

"Then what is it?"

"Look, I get this place is special to you. But it's not real life. It's nostalgia. A vacation from what actually matters."

"That's where you're wrong." Her voice was low and tight. "For some of us, this is the only place that ever felt real."

We were quiet for a long moment.

Finally, Brynn spoke. "When I was seventeen, I spent a whole summer here. My dad had just left, and my mom was—" She stopped. "I hated everything. But Dove Key made me feel like I could be someone different. I think everyone needs a place like that. Even you."

I tried to say something glib, but I couldn't. The idea unsettled me, almost worse than her panic underwater.

After the boat docked, we gathered our things and stepped off, waving goodbye to Eli. The walk back from the pier was quiet, and without discussion, we continued, strolling along the tide line. Brynn hugged the towel around her shoulders, her steps small and sure beside me. She glanced at me every few paces, like she was trying to solve an equation.

"Thanks again," she said finally, her voice low. "For not letting me drown."

"You're welcome," I said. The lack of a sarcastic follow-up hung in the air between us.

Then, before I could process it, her fingers found mine. It wasn't a gesture for an audience. Her hand was small and cool, her grip tentative at first, then a little firmer.

My first instinct was to pull away. But I didn't. I laced my fingers through hers, the contact sending a current straight up my arm. This wasn't part of the plan. Yet we started walking again, our linked hands swinging gently between us.

"So," she said, her tone turning playful, "now that you've saved my life, does that mean I owe you a favor?"

I squeezed her hand. "I think the traditional boon is a new sports car, but I'll settle for you admitting I'm a superior fake boyfriend."

She laughed. "Don't push it, Mercer. You're currently in second place, right behind the guy from that movie who pretends to be a coma patient."

"Ouch. I don't know if my acting skills are up to faking a coma."

"You could practice," she said, swinging our hands higher. "I'll bring you grapes at the hospital to tempt you."

We walked on, the easy rhythm of our steps and the warm weight of her hand in mine feeling dangerously natural. For a few minutes, I let myself feel it—the simple warmth, the effortless back-and-forth, the feeling of standing next to someone and not needing to pretend.

Until I realized how terrifying it all was.

This was how it started. The small, quiet moments that build into something you couldn't control, something you couldn't walk away from without leaving a part of yourself behind.

I gently pulled my hand away and jammed it into my pocket. "We should probably get back. Don't want to be late for whatever mandatory fun Holly and Harper have planned for us tonight."

Brynn's smile faltered for a second, but she recovered quickly, nodding as she started walking again. The easy warmth between us was gone, replaced by the familiar, safer distance of our charade.

I fell into step beside her. For a few minutes, holding her hand along the beach, I'd forgotten it was all a game. Just a way to pass time until I could get back to real life. But it was getting harder to remember what that was supposed to be.

Chapter Three

BRYNN

THE REHEARSAL DINNER was held on the sand behind Sunset Siesta, where linen-draped tables stood just above the high tide line and tiki torches flickered in the dark. A gentle ocean breeze fluttered napkins and tangled my hair into a briny halo. It looked like the set of a travel show, complete with an acoustic guitarist and enough citrusy cocktails to tranquilize a village.

Just an hour ago, we'd all stood on the lovely salt-and-pepper beach for the actual rehearsal, a clumsy, giggly affair orchestrated by a cheerful, flip-flop-wearing officiant. As maid of honor, I'd walked down the sandy aisle on Dean's arm, a moment of public intimacy that felt both ridiculously fake and dangerously real. He stood beside Josh at the makeshift altar, looking handsome and out of place in a T-shirt and shorts, his expression a perfect mask of best-man solemnity. We practiced our entrance and exit, the whole performance a masterclass in pretending. I was still buzzing from the effort.

I hovered at the edge of the event, trying to look like I belonged. My black dress—borrowed from Holly and one size too optimistic—clung to the sweat on my lower back. My name card had been bedazzled, ensuring I'd be visible from the moon. An entire table of relatives stared at me with the intensity of people who'd once changed my diapers and never moved on.

Dean slid into the seat beside me, setting down two sweating tumblers of sangria and a plate of conch fritters. His button-down sleeves were rolled to display the muscle of his forearms, and his hair was neatly combed. His cologne found me—a spicy, expensive scent that blended with the salt air and that I couldn't help inhaling.

He draped an arm over the back of my chair, his thumb skimming my shoulder blades. "Now it looks like you're the one plotting an escape."

I sipped the sangria and tried not to lean into his touch. Tried not to remember that moment of connection when we strolled along this same beach a few hours ago. "I'm deciding between swimming to Cuba or faking my own death. You?"

"If you bolted, they'd send out a search party. Your cousin is conducting a headcount every five minutes."

I stifled a groan. "My family doesn't handle unpredictability well."

He leaned closer, a shadow of a smile on his lips. "And yet here you are, courting chaos."

"If by chaos you mean deep-fried seafood and unrelenting social exposure, then yes." I tossed a conch fritter in his direction. "Or maybe you meant chaos of the Dean Mercer variety?"

He caught it in his teeth. After chewing and swallowing, he winked. "I'll keep that mystery. Speaking of mysteries, I was reading in the dive shop earlier. Did you know a group of jellyfish is called a smack?"

"No one on Earth except Eli knows that, Dean. And I promise you, no one but him cares," I added, unable to suppress a laugh.

He flashed that smile again. "That's why I like you, Brynn. You can't be intimidated by raw intellect."

His easy confidence, the casual way he crowded my space, made it hard to remember we were pretending. He played the part so well I was starting to believe it.

The table slowly filled. Holly and Josh beamed, accompanied by an assortment of family and friends, and at least two people who looked ready to initiate a group icebreaker at any moment. Dean's arm stayed where it was.

The woman across from us—one of Holly's coworkers —leaned in. "So, how did you two meet?"

Dean didn't miss a beat. "Book club."

I nearly inhaled a cherry tomato.

"Book club?" she repeated.

Dean nodded. "Brynn's into the classics. I was there for the snacks. Turns out we both hate the ending of *The Great Gatsby*, and the rest is history."

I picked it up from there, swept up in his ridiculous energy as I stroked a finger over that granite jaw. "He pretended to have strong opinions about Fitzgerald's symbolism, but I'm pretty sure he was just in it for the scandalous affair."

The woman laughed, charmed. "That's adorable."

"Yeah, I'm a sucker for a happy ending," Dean said, his gaze on me as if I were the only one at the table.

My chest fizzed, and I had to glance away. Was this how it felt to be genuinely adored, even for show? My ex would have made a PowerPoint on codependency, but with the warm weight of Dean's presence, this felt more like a release.

The next hour was a blur of grilled shrimp and escalating banter. I managed to grab Holly for thirty seconds by the bar, giving her the lightning-fast version of our hastily arranged fake relationship. Her eyes lit up with the same gleam she used to get before we TP'd the principal's house in tenth grade. She was in. From her seat at the head table, she watched our performance with the keen interest of a director, loving every second of my escape from Aunt Carol's clutches.

Dean made the charade easy. He murmured jokes in my ear, the heat of his breath sending tingles down my neck, then delivered anecdotes with deadpan sincerity. Every time someone looked skeptical, he'd raise my hand to his lips and brush a kiss over my knuckles. The move was so smooth it made me lightheaded.

I should have hated how good he was at this. Instead, I watched him from the corner of my eye, cataloging the lines bracketing his smile, that damn dimple in his left cheek. He'd see me staring and shoot me a wink, as if he'd caught me in a secret.

When dessert arrived—a Key lime pie with a layer of meringue so thick it looked like insulation—Dean and I both reached for the same slice. His fingers closed around mine for a second. Not a staged gesture, but a brief, grounding squeeze. My pulse tripped over itself.

He let go with a smile and passed me the pie. "Ladies first."

Holly's voice snapped me out of my trance. "Brynn, you've got to tell everyone about the karaoke contest!"

My ears turned pink. "Oh, that was nothing. I might have been a little drunk."

Dean jumped in. He'd actually been there back in

Atlanta last year. "She's being modest. She has an entire routine to 'Total Eclipse of the Heart.' There were props. Though I don't think she's planning a repeat performance. Sorry, folks."

The table dissolved into laughter. I loved the way he could redirect the spotlight to himself when he sensed I needed it.

The sun set, and the tiki torches flickered brighter. People paired off to stroll the beach. Dean and I sat for a long time, picking at the remains of the meal, not needing to talk.

The wind had cooled, and goosebumps rose on my skin. Dean removed his jacket and placed it over my shoulders, his spicy male scent surrounding me and making me feel drunk. He pulled his chair closer until our knees touched, then caught a loose strand of my hair and tucked it behind my ear.

"Convincing performance, Ms. Vance," he said softly.

I didn't trust myself to answer. I offered him the last bite of pie. The fork scraped the plate, the sound oddly intimate in the hush. I'd started the evening expecting to endure the charade, but now I wished it wouldn't end.

"You realize we're winning this, right?" He leaned in, his voice low.

"Winning what?"

"The game. They all believe it." His eyes met mine, sharp and sure. "But you don't have to keep pretending if you don't want to."

The gentle, open way he said it broke through my last defense.

"Maybe I don't want to."

He smiled, slow and soft, and for a heartbeat, I felt lighter than I had in years.

Someone turned up the music. The first notes of a love song drifted across the sand.

Dean stood and held out his hand. "Dance with me, beautiful lady."

My heart tripped again, and I let him lead me toward the lights. The old dread in my chest was replaced by something fragile and bright. A maybe, shimmering just out of reach. I squeezed his hand. He squeezed back.

For the first time, I let myself hope it wasn't an act.

The sand was cool beneath my bare toes as we reached the impromptu dance floor. A live band slid into a slow, honeyed version of "At Last." Holly and Josh swayed at the center, a tangle of arms and affection. Dean swept his arms around me, and my lungs forgot how to operate.

"Ever danced barefoot?" he asked.

"I've taught first grade for three years. If you count the Macarena at school assemblies, I'm an expert."

He grinned and drew me in, his palm finding the small of my back. The contact was solid, not tentative. When he tugged me close, it was like he knew the shape of my body. I went willingly, stumbling a little as my foot dug into the sand. He caught my balance without a blink.

"Relax," he whispered against my hairline. "You're allowed to have fun."

I tried, but every cell in me was alert. The warmth of his chest seeped through his shirt. I looked up at the faint shadow of stubble on his jaw, a tiny scar at his temple. He stared down at me, blue eyes framed by long lashes. The whole tableau felt as delicate as a snow globe. Like a single, honest word would break it.

We settled into a loose rhythm. The sand under me shifted, and I kept fumbling toward him, catching myself on his shoulder.

"You're terrible at this," he murmured, his lips brushing my ear.

My lips curled of their own accord. "I warned you. I peaked at 'Three Blind Mice.'"

He laughed, the sound sending a fresh rush of goosebumps down my arms. His hand tightened at my waist. My own hands had nowhere to go, so I clung to his shirt, fingers curling into the soft cotton. It was too intimate for two people pretending.

"So, what's our backstory now?" I asked. "Still paddleboard yoga and book club?"

He turned us in a slow circle. "Let's keep them guessing. Next time, we'll say we met on a serial killer podcast forum."

"Wow. You really know how to sweep a girl off her feet."

Dean smiled, slow and wicked. "Who says I haven't?"

My heart hammered in my throat.

A couple of songs passed. I was giddy, spun out on alcohol and his closeness, and the way he never got bored of making me laugh. The crowd seemed happy to let us exist in our own little bubble.

The next song was a ballad. Dean drew me closer, my chest pressed to his, my cheek brushing his collar. I felt the steady thump of his heart. He smelled of sweat, salt, and aftershave, and I was in danger of being completely, pathetically lost in it.

In other words, it was the perfect time for Aunt Carol to materialize, martini in hand, her smile beaming and intensely curious. She didn't circle like a shark. She floated over, inserting herself into our bubble with the cheerful entitlement of a beloved relative.

"Well, look at you two!" she chirped, her voice carrying

over the music. "Brynn, darling, I haven't seen you this happy in ages."

I tensed, but Dean just smiled, never breaking our rhythm. "She has that effect on me. I'd like to think the feeling is mutual."

Aunt Carol's smile didn't waver, but her eyes sharpened. "It's all so sudden, though! How long have you been keeping this handsome man a secret from your favorite aunt?"

The question was a direct hit, designed to catch me off guard. My cheeks heated.

"Oh, it's… it's pretty new," I stammered, the lie feeling flimsy on my tongue.

"New is right!" Aunt Carol said with a little laugh, patting my arm. "Poor Todd was so surprised. But it must be the real deal if you're already this inseparable." She took a deliberate sip of her martini, her gaze flicking between us. "You two just look so in love!"

The words hung in the air, a challenge disguised as a compliment. I felt the eyes from nearby tables on us. Dean tensed beside me, the steady rhythm of our dance faltering.

Dean's expression shifted. He stared directly at me, his gaze serious, intent. "I think we can do better than just *looking* the part." His voice was just loud enough for our audience to hear.

Then, without warning, he spun me, caught me at the waist, and dipped me low over the sand. I yelped, unprepared, arms windmilling until I found his shoulders and clung for dear life.

The world tilted. Torchlight and stars above, Dean's face so close I saw the flecks in his light-blue eyes. My hand moved down to his chest, settling above his wildly beating heart. Everything stilled—the music, the chatter, the crash of the surf.

He waited, searching my face. His eyes stopped on my mouth. My brain was all static.

Then he kissed me.

When the heat of his mouth hit mine, the bottom dropped out of everything. His lips were gentler than I expected, cautious at first, giving me an out. I didn't take it. I pressed up to meet him, and he deepened the kiss, his hand at the nape of my neck.

He deepened the kiss, his fingers tangling in my hair as he tilted my head back. His thumb traced slow, maddening circles on my skin while his other arm held me against him. A soft groan rumbled in his chest, and then his tongue traced the seam of my lips, a hot, wet demand for more.

I opened for him without a second thought. He swept inside, tasting of IPA and salt and something that was just *him*. Mindful of where we were, he withdrew to a more proper but still head-spinning kiss. His stubble scraped against my chin, and I wanted more.

I wanted everything.

My fingers, which had been braced on his shoulders, twisted into the fabric of his shirt, clutching him closer as if I could pull him inside me.

I forgot where we were. I forgot the music, the crowd, the tiki torches. There was only the slick heat of his mouth, the possessive grip of his hand in my hair, and the stunning realization that this felt more real than anything I had felt in years.

Then the world roared back all at once—conversation, laughter, the music. Our lips parted, but Dean didn't let go. Not until I opened my eyes and he smiled like he'd just solved the world's most impossible equation.

He righted me gently. Aunt Carol was nowhere to be seen. The moment was ours.

Dean ran a thumb along my cheek, his smile softer than I'd ever seen it. "Are you okay?"

I was not okay, but I nodded. I wanted to do it again.

Instead, I leaned my forehead against his chest, letting the music carry us a little longer.

"Next time," I said, my voice shaky as we resumed our dance, "warn me before you go full-on *Dancing with the Stars*."

He laughed, his body vibrating under my hands. "Where's the fun in that?"

I smiled. For the rest of the song, I let myself be held, swaying in the dark with someone who made me feel like the past didn't have to dictate the future. The song ended, and reality edged in. But for those few minutes, I'd forgotten what I was supposed to be afraid of.

And when Dean stared back at me, I saw it—he'd forgotten, too.

"Let's get a drink." I nodded toward the tiki bar, desperate for a change of scenery, for something to do with my hands.

"Good idea," he said, his voice a little rough. He didn't let go immediately. Instead, his hand slid from my waist to the small of my back, a warm, guiding pressure as we walked away from the dance floor together. The gesture was so natural, so proprietary, it made my heart thump even harder.

We didn't speak on the way to the bar. We didn't have to. The air between us was electric, charged with everything that had just happened and everything that might happen next.

The bartender took one look at our dazed expressions and reached for the rum. "Two Hurricanes?"

"Make mine a double." I gripped the bamboo counter for support.

Dean stood beside me, so close our arms brushed. He didn't look at me, just stared straight ahead at the rows of liquor bottles, but I could feel the tension radiating off him. He hadn't been acting. I was sure of it.

The drinks arrived. I took a long, desperate swallow of mine, the rum scorching a path down my throat. It did nothing to calm the frantic energy buzzing under my skin. The memory of his lips—gentle, then demanding, then *wow*—was the kind of kiss that made you forget your own name, never mind the rules of a fake relationship.

I risked a glance at him. He was studying me, his expression unreadable in the flickering torchlight. He hadn't touched his drink.

"So," he said, his voice low. "That was… convincing."

"It was a tactical decision." I tried to reclaim the safety of our joke.

His mouth twitched into a half-smile, but his eyes were serious. "Right. Tactical." He finally picked up his glass, swirling the dark liquid. "We should probably get back out there. Keep up appearances."

He was offering me an out, a chance to pretend that kiss hadn't just rewired my entire nervous system. I could take it. We could go back to the dance floor, back to the safety of the charade.

But as the party hummed behind us, I made a silent vow—no more pretending, not to myself. If I was going to risk getting hurt, it might as well be for something that made me feel this alive.

I met his gaze and held it. "Or we could just stay here for a minute. Alone."

He watched me for a long beat, searching my face.

Then, a smile spread across his lips—a small, private thing just for us.

Not a challenge. An invitation.

"Yeah." His shoulders relaxed at last. "I'd like that."

He turned back to the bar, our shoulders touching. We drank together, the joy of the party a distant hum. For the first time in forever, I didn't feel like a visitor in my own life. I felt wildly, dangerously out of control. It was the scariest, most hopeful feeling in the world.

Chapter Four

DEAN

I'D HEARD of the walk of shame, but nobody warned me about the brunch of existential crisis. At 9:58 a.m., I sat across from Brynn in the Driftwood Grill's dining room. My eggs had congealed into an interpretive sculpture. Her fruit cup sweated in the Florida humidity. We hadn't made eye contact since we sat down.

Maybe she hoped last night's detonation on the dance floor could be swept under a rug of mimosas and buffet bacon. Maybe I was, too. But the more I tried to push it aside, the more it ballooned, crowding the air between us until every fork scrape felt like a personal insult. It was just a kiss, right? Just a fake kiss I'd spent half the night revisiting, analyzing, and yearning to repeat.

"You going to eat that or just rearrange it for the next forty-five minutes?" Brynn's voice sliced through the silence.

I poked my eggs. "I'm letting them age. Adds complexity."

She snorted. "In a hundred years, they'll find these and think it's a crime scene."

I risked a glance. Brynn's hair was down today, hiding part of her face in soft waves. Her gorgeous eyes were half-mast. She looked tired in a way that made my chest hurt.

"Do you think it's weird that weddings always do these forced group meals?" she asked, her eyes tracking a family squabbling over the last sticky bun. "Like we're all prisoners of love, serving time at Table Seven."

"It's a cult, and mimosas are the Kool-Aid." I took a sip of my own, realizing my hand was shaking. "It's fine. I can fake being social for an hour."

"I can't." She pressed her palms flat to the table. "Which is why I'm planning a jailbreak."

A spark of hope ignited. "Go on."

"I saw a sign by the pier for a half-day fishing charter," she said. "Austin Coleridge is the captain here. We could be somewhere that isn't here. I know Austin—he's practically the fish whisperer."

I almost kissed her again, this time out of pure gratitude. "I'd risk open water for you, Vance."

"Let's do it, then." She gathered her bag. "Meet you at the pier in fifteen?"

I was on my feet before she finished. I left a twenty under my uneaten eggs and followed her out, feeling the stares of wedding guests in my wake. When we passed the bride-to-be, she cocked her head at Brynn. Brynn gave a tiny tilt of her head, and Holly's lips curved in a knowing smile. I pretended not to notice.

The wooden pier was already baking in the midmorning sun. I spotted the guy who had to be Austin Coleridge at the end of the dock. His arms were crossed, his navy work shirt tight over muscles that could probably deadlift a small whale. His face was unreadable, and his stubbly dark beard matched his hair.

He nodded as we approached. "Good to see you again, Brynn. And—Dean, right?"

"Mercer," I said, sticking out a hand.

Austin sized me up, then gave my hand a single, surgical shake. "You ever fish?"

"My grandfather took me once when I was eight. I dropped the bait bucket overboard and cried."

Brynn laughed, and the tension in her shoulders eased. "Don't worry. Austin won't let you near the bait."

"I try to run a respectable operation," Austin deadpanned, ushering us aboard. The boat was pristine—fiberglass scrubbed to a dull shine, rods lined up like soldiers, the deck uncluttered except for a battered cooler and two bait boxes.

Brynn moved with easy familiarity, dropping her bag near the bow and scanning the tackle. "You always have the latest and greatest, don't you, Austin?"

"Don't touch my gear," he said with a twitch of his lips. He glanced at me, then back to her. "Weather's perfect. Gulls are out. If we're lucky, we'll catch something worth exaggerating later."

I slid onto the nearest bench, suddenly aware of how out of place I was in my dry-cleaned polo and boat shoes. Brynn, by contrast, fit the deck like it was made for her. The women I was usually attracted to were polished and performative. Brynn wasn't trying to look cute or impress anyone. Having traded her sundress for cutoffs and a resort T-shirt, she was confident in a way that had nothing to do with a job title or bank account. It was a quiet self-assurance I hadn't encountered before, and it was ridiculously alluring. She leaned against the rail, face tipped to the sun. I tried to memorize the moment—the wind tangling her hair, the line of her jaw, the faint smile that made me want to abandon ship.

I tore my gaze away and tried to get a metaphorical grip.

Austin started the engines, and the boat eased away from the dock. He stood at the helm, legs braced, his focus absolute. Barefoot, Brynn clambered over the deck, reeling in loose lines.

She tossed me a life vest with a smirk. "You've got the city-boy look down. You might want to wear that."

Laughing, I tossed it back to her. "Oh, shut up."

We cruised past the breakwater into an endless sheet of blue. Gulls shadowed the wake. The sun made the water shimmer so bright it felt like looking into the future—featureless, blinding, and full of hazards.

Brynn plopped down beside me, her knee knocking mine. "You look green."

"Motion sickness or nerves. Hard to say."

She laughed, softer this time. "It's just a boat ride, Dean."

Easy for her to say. For me, it felt like a trial by saltwater, with two judges—one immune to bullshit, the other immune to my charms. Though I kept trying to warm her up to them.

Out in open water, Austin throttled down. "I'll set the lines. You two can handle drinks."

Brynn trotted to the cooler to remove a soda, then tossed me a second. I fumbled the catch.

Austin lifted one brow. "You sure you're up for this?"

I popped the tab. "If I puke, it's only because I'm enjoying myself so much."

Brynn snorted. "He's fine, Austin. Don't let the land-lubber exterior fool you."

Austin grunted and turned to the rods. I studied him,

how deliberate and natural every movement was, how the sea seemed to obey him. I envied his steadiness. Meanwhile, every glance at Brynn reminded me of how unmoored I felt.

Brynn finished her soda and tossed the empty in the trash. She glanced at me, searching my face. "Seriously, you okay?"

I had no idea how to answer that. "Yeah. Just getting my sea legs."

"The footing feels a little uneven, doesn't it?" As soon as the words left her mouth, our eyes collided and held fast. She felt it too, that buzz between us neither would acknowledge out loud.

Austin throttled back and the engine softened to a low rumble. He jerked his chin at Brynn. "You remember how to bait a line?"

She grinned. "Bet I remember better than you do."

They had the easy rapport of old conspirators. I saw a version of Brynn I hadn't met yet. A little tougher, a little wilder. Again, the ground shifted under my feet.

My line snagged twice before I managed to get the bait into the water. Brynn watched, biting back a smile.

"If you stare at it, nothing happens," she said, settling onto the bow. "Try ignoring it. Fish hate a try-hard."

Austin snorted as he leaned casually against the console. He studied me for a long minute, as if deciding whether I was salvageable. "I grew up thinking people were like fish. Spook easy, bite at anything shiny, mostly just want to be left alone. But the good ones—you have to earn their trust. Takes patience."

"Or chum," I said.

He grinned, brief, sharp, then gone. "That too."

As we drifted, the rhythm of the boat and the sun's heat worked a slow anesthetic on my nerves. After a while,

I forgot to care how I looked. My shoulders dropped and my stomach settled. I let the sun melt the rest of my defenses.

Austin, who had been silently watching the lines, turned his attention to me. "What's your line of work back in the city? When you're not crashing weddings, I mean."

"Finance," I replied, the word feeling hollow out here. "I'm a Certified Financial Planner, but now I work as a futures analyst for a big investment firm."

Austin nodded slowly, his face giving nothing away. "Sounds important."

"It's mostly just moving decimals around on a computer screen," I admitted. "I used to do financial planning with families and small businesses. Helped them prepare for the future and enjoy the present, you know?"

"I know a little about running a business," Austin said, a hint of dry humor in his voice.

"I liked it more in some ways," I continued, the thought forming as I spoke. "It felt like I was actually impacting people's lives, not just a balance sheet."

Brynn, who had been quietly listening from the bow, wandered over. She nudged my arm, a knowing glint in her eyes. "Careful, Mercer. You're starting to sound like you've got itchy feet, too."

I immediately put my guard back up, shrugging off the observation. "Nah. The money's too good to walk away from."

She didn't push, just gave me a small, perceptive smile before turning back to her fishing rod. But she was right, of course. I hadn't thought about it in a while, but watching Austin—a guy who ran his business with his own two hands, who answered to no one but the tides— stirred something in me. The idea of having my own shingle, a small CFP firm helping people like Austin and other small businesses, had a certain appeal. An image of me with a shop on Main Street under one of those ridiculous ornate lampposts flashed before me, and I almost laughed.

Yeah, right…

A frown lowered my lips as I tested the line for a vibration. Nothing. I eased out a long sigh.

Brynn handed me a fresh can of soda. "You know, you're allowed to enjoy this. It's not a test."

I rolled the can between my palms. "I'm not good at things I can't win."

She raised an eyebrow. "You really think everything's a competition?"

"Not everything. Just the stuff that matters."

"And what matters?"

I was saved from answering by a shout from Austin. "Brynn! You're up."

She scrambled to the stern and hauled on the rod, muscles flexing as she wrestled with whatever was on the other end. The fish was a good one—a speckled snapper, scales iridescent in the sun. Brynn whooped as she landed it, and Austin clapped her on the back before letting it slip back into the water.

She collapsed onto the bench next to me, grinning. "Your turn. Catch something, or I'll never let you hear the end of it."

My line hung slack, utterly ignored. Brynn giggled and reached over to adjust the drag on my reel, her hands warm and sure.

Austin called from the bow, "Let it run next time. Don't overthink it."

"Good advice for life?" I muttered.

Brynn heard me. "You could stand to relax a little."

"I'll take that under advisement."

Her eyes turned serious. "Why are you so cynical, Dean?"

The question landed like a thrown anchor. I was too tired to fake it. "It's not life I'm cynical about. It's expectations. The idea that anyone ever gets it right."

"Gets what right?"

Love… that feeling when you look into someone's eyes and feel like you're home.

But I could never say that out loud. "Weddings drag up all sorts of crap, don't they?"

"Did someone hurt you?" Her voice was gentle, not prying.

And I had no idea why, but with Austin at the other end of the boat and no witnesses but the placid blue ocean, the truth came out. "Once. I was an idiot—thought if I just loved hard enough, everything would work out. She left. Said she wanted more adventure in her life. I wasn't it." Just saying the words out loud and remembering that time made my skin crawl.

Brynn listened, never looking away. There was no pity in her expression, just quiet understanding.

"So now you keep everyone at arm's length," she said, not unkindly.

"Safer that way." I shook off the bad memory with a determined effort.

She nodded. "Does it work?"

I laughed, surprised by the truth. "Not always."

She nudged me with her shoulder, smiling. "You might be more of a romantic than you let on, Mercer."

I wanted to argue, but I couldn't. It felt good to admit defeat to her.

Austin shouted, "Dean, reel in. We're heading back."

Brynn gave my arm a parting squeeze, then bounded off to help him. I sat there and worked the reel, the wind drying the sweat from my face, feeling lighter than I had any right to. When I glanced over, Brynn was watching me. She held my gaze for a long, unguarded moment, then winked.

As Austin steered us home, I stared at Brynn and thought, *Maybe it's not about winning. Maybe it's about finding someone who makes you want to try.*

After we docked, Brynn insisted on treating me to ice cream to make up for getting personal. Which was a good idea since I was still trying to figure out why I'd opened up to a woman I'd only thought of as a distant friend and schoolmarm a few days ago. Before I knew she was fun, smart, and yeah, I had to admit it, sexy.

We thoroughly scrubbed our hands before heading down Main Street, which a 50s television show would have envied—quaint shops, colorful awnings, and huge balls of hanging flowers. Brynn promised that the Corner Scoop wielded a Key lime cone of such ferocity it would knock me over.

The ice cream shop looked like a postcard—all pale blue walls, seashell garlands, and a counter covered in snapshots of kids with sticky faces. It smelled of sugar and nostalgia. I had to remind myself I hated this shit.

The moment we stepped inside, Brynn changed. The slight tension coiled in her shoulders since returning to dry land dissolved under the blast of frigid air conditioning. Her steps became more confident. She ran a hand along the worn countertop like she was greeting an old friend, a small smile gracing her lips. I'd pegged her as having soft edges, but in here, she looked solid. Like she was made of the same stuff as the foundation of this place.

Behind the counter stood a woman with steel-gray hair and arms that could bench-press the ice cream machine.

She took one look at Brynn and hollered, "Well, if it isn't my runaway girl!"

Brynn laughed. "Hi, Doris. Still serving the best brain freeze in the Keys?"

"Always for you." Doris shimmied around the counter and enveloped Brynn in a hug that could double as CPR. "Well, hello there, Mr. Tall Drink of Water." She fixed me with a shrewd gaze. "Hope you've got a sweet tooth."

I nodded, suddenly twelve, and tried not to fidget. "I'll try anything once."

"That's what they all say," Doris said, winking, then squeezed Brynn's shoulder. "But this one is the real deal. Worked here the summer she turned seventeen. Best scooper I ever had—except for her tragic lack of upper body strength."

"Some of us are built for brains, not biceps," Brynn retorted.

I laughed out loud, enjoying myself immensely.

"We'll both take the Dove Key lime cone," Brynn said as she bumped my hip.

"You got it, honey." Doris slid back the glass top of a freezer and put a bicep bigger than mine to work.

"I swear, that time was the easiest I ever breathed." A wistful note entered Brynn's voice as she swept her gaze around the shop. "Teaching is my passion, but that summer was just pure, simple fun. No lesson plans, just scoops."

"Mmm-hmm." Doris scooped the second cone. "Lesson plans, huh? You became a teacher?"

"First grade." Brynn's smile widened. "I'm really glad to see you're still behind the counter here."

"As much as I hate to admit it, I'm not getting any younger." Doris leaned on the counter. "I'm thinking about selling this place."

The words dropped like a bowling ball. Brynn blinked. "Seriously?"

"It's time. But I won't sell to just anyone. This place is family. Needs someone who gets it." She looked directly at Brynn as she handed her both cones. "Ever thought about running an ice cream shop, honey?"

Brynn fumbled one, and I caught it deftly. Her face, which had already taken on a golden hue from the sun, paled. "Me? I'm a teacher, Doris. I wouldn't know where to start."

Doris wagged a finger. "You ran this place by yourself more than I did that summer. You've got the touch with people. This place needs heart, not a business plan. Just something to think about."

For a second, Brynn looked like a kid caught between the promise of Christmas and the terror of asking for what she wanted most.

I said, without thinking, "You'd be great at it." Brynn looked at me like I'd spoken in tongues. I pressed on. "Seriously. You're organized, people love you, and you already know the secret handshakes around here. You belong."

Doris barked her approval. "I like this one, Brynn. He's got good sense."

Brynn colored but didn't look away from me. "You really think I could do it?"

"Yeah. I do." I said the words softly, but I meant every one. The woman before me could do damn near anything from what I'd seen.

She nodded slowly, tucking the thought away. Doris patted the counter twice with her hand. "On the house. For old times' sake."

We sat at a sun-faded table and ate our cones. Brynn was lost in thought, the possibilities ricocheting behind her eyes. I stayed quiet, content to be a bystander to her happiness. And she was right. The ice cream was the perfect mix of tart and sweet. The waffle cone balanced both perfectly.

When we left, Doris called after us, "Don't be strangers!"

Outside, the afternoon was soft and sticky. Brynn licked a trail of melting ice cream from her wrist. "Thank you. For… all of that."

I shrugged, feeling exposed. "Just telling the truth."

"That's rare these days."

When we got back to Sunset Siesta, we strolled along the pier. Both boats we'd been on, *Sunset Diver* and *Line Dancer*, bobbed gently on either side, ready for tomorrow's adventures.

Brynn stopped and gazed at the distant horizon. "I don't know what I want, Dean. I just know I want something different."

I forgot to breathe as the sun caught her eyes, illuminating the gold in them. And I realized I wanted to be the one to help her find it. I was a man who didn't believe in love, and that wasn't what this was—not after only a few days. But it felt like something had started between us.

We were silent as we strolled back to the resort, hand in hand. Sometimes, words only got in the way.

Chapter Five

BRYNN

THE RECEPTION WAS in full swing, a joyful tumble of clinking glasses and fairy lights strung over Sunset Siesta's beach. Alone for a moment, I sat at the head table with a champagne flute in hand and took my first real breath of the day. The ceremony just down the beach had been beautiful, our toasts funny and heartfelt, and I had managed to get through my own speech without ugly-crying. Now, finally, with all the public-facing duties over, I could just be.

From my vantage point, I observed the happy couple. Holly and Josh were surrounded by admirers, lost in their own universe. My gaze drifted to the starlit tropical sky. It was absurd how much I didn't want the trip to end.

I had a perfect view of Dean. He was circulating with a glass of whiskey in hand, effortlessly playing the charming Best Man—laughing with a group of Josh's college friends, gracefully dodging a bridesmaid who was clearly on the hunt, even enduring a back-slapping hug from Holly's uncle. He excelled at being exactly what the moment required. A pang of something I refused to name—envy, longing—twisted in my gut.

That line of thought ended with a thud when Todd Peterson sat across from me, clutching a plate of potato salad and looking like he'd spent the night fighting off wild dogs.

"Hi, Brynn," he said glumly.

"Hey, Todd. You doing okay?"

He picked at his salad. "I think there's Miracle Whip in this. I'm more of a mayo guy."

"Rough."

"Anyway, I wanted to say sorry if I was too forward the other night. Carol confirmed you have a boyfriend."

I could have let him dangle, but he looked genuinely miserable. "Yes, I do. It's okay, Todd. We're all doing our best."

He brightened a bit. "Yeah. Well, Carol's taking me back to Atlanta tomorrow morning."

I didn't know what to say to that. "Safe travels, okay?"

He rose to his feet like a limp noodle. "You, too. Good luck with the boyfriend thing. He seems nice."

Todd shuffled off, then detoured to explain to a baffled wedding guest that the reception's spotty Wi-Fi was likely due to interference from the kitchen's commercial microwaves. I exhaled a deep sigh. That chapter, at least, was closed.

I stared absently at the pier and its bobbing boats. I would return to Atlanta the day after tomorrow. But here, with the salt air in my lungs, I felt brave enough to imagine a different future. One with Dean? That might be a stretch, but tempting. Then another future flitted through my mind.

Doris's words from yesterday echoed. *"Ever thought about running an ice cream shop, honey?"*

I'd dismissed it as another risk I wasn't built for. But the memory of standing in the Scoop, the easy confidence I felt there… it was the one time this trip I felt at home. What if my life wasn't about finding someone, but about building something? The thought was so big, so audacious, it made my pulse quicken. It was the scariest, most exciting idea I'd had in years.

A shadow fell across my table, pulling me back from my thoughts. Dean appeared, wearing a frown. With a sigh, he dropped into Todd's empty seat and stared at the plate. He raised his head and arched a dark brow. "Did I just witness a breakup?"

"Only if you count Miracle Whip as a dealbreaker."

"I don't trust anything with that many syllables." He smiled, something softening behind his eyes. For a moment, we were just two people, not actors in a farce. The thought was exhilarating and terrifying.

The DJ started the first dance. Holly and Josh swayed, lost in their own universe. I felt a pang of envy at how easy they made it look.

Dean followed my gaze. "You ever think about it?"

"This? Getting married?" I shrugged, forcing a laugh. "Maybe in another life."

He studied me. "What's stopping you?"

I wanted to tell him the truth—that I'd spent so long making myself small and safe that wanting more felt like a crime. That I was tired of playing it safe but didn't know how to stop. Instead, I said, "I guess I never met the right guy."

Dean grinned, lazy and wicked. "That's a low bar, Vance."

"You'd be surprised."

He reached across the table, his fingers brushing mine, so brief I could pretend it didn't happen. We sat like that for a while, the music wrapping around us. For the first time in a long time, I wasn't restless or looking for an exit. I was just present, accepting what might come.

Dean stood, pulling me up by the hand. "Come on. Let's make some bad decisions."

Laughing, I let him lead me to the dance floor, my hand warm in his. The night, and all its possibilities, awaited.

The DJ transitioned from an upbeat party track to a slow, sultry love song with a heavy bass line that vibrated through the sand and into my bones. Dean pulled me into his arms, his hand confidently resting on the small of my back. We fell into an easy rhythm, our bodies swaying together.

"Having fun yet?" I murmured, my lips close to his ear.

His hand tightened, pulling me flush against him. I could feel the hard planes of his chest and the solid strength in his thighs.

"I'm starting to see the appeal of these things." His voice was a low vibration against my cheek. "The open bar helps."

"Just the open bar?" I teased, letting my hands wander from his shoulders to the back of his neck, my fingers playing with the soft hair at his nape. His breath hitched, a tiny sound that sent a thrill through me.

"Okay, maybe the company isn't so bad either," he admitted, his gaze dropping to my mouth. "You feel incredible in my arms, Brynn."

The directness of it stole my breath. "Being your fake girlfriend is a tough job. But someone has to do it."

His eyes darkened, the blue turning to a deep, stormy cobalt. The air between us crackled, thick with the memory of our last kiss and the unspoken promise of the next one. This wasn't for show anymore. We both knew it.

"We're still on duty, right?" he murmured as he maneuvered us to a more dimly lit section. "We have to make it look convincing for the audience."

He leaned in and captured my mouth in a slow, deliberate kiss. There was no pretense of performance. It was pure desire. His lips were firm and confident, moving over mine with an ease that made my knees weak. He tasted of whiskey and salt, the intoxicating flavor of a man who knew exactly what he was doing.

When he pulled back, I was breathless, my lips tingling. I looked up at him through my lashes, a slow, wicked smile spreading across my face. "Absolutely. Can't let our audience down, can we?"

Before he could react, I initiated the next kiss, rising on my toes to meet him. I slanted my mouth over his, my tongue swiping against his bottom lip, a bold invitation he answered immediately. He groaned, a low, guttural sound, and opened for me, our tongues tangling in a heated dance. It was a kiss that spoke of long nights and messed sheets, a kiss between two people who were done playing games.

The music was a distant thrum, a bassline for the beat of my heart. Dean's hand slid from the small of my back, his fingers tracing a fiery path up my side until his thumb brushed the curve of my breast. I gasped into his mouth, the shock of pleasure so intense my hips instinctively pressed closer, seeking more. I could feel the hard ridge of his erection against my thigh, undeniable proof of what this was doing to both of us. My hands, which had gripped his hair, slid down his neck, my nails grazing his skin. He shuddered.

The song faded, the final notes hanging in the humid

air like a held breath. He pulled me in for one last, deep kiss that had nothing to do with rhythm or romance and everything to do with raw, possessive hunger.

When we broke apart, we were both breathing heavily. The rest of the party was a blurry constellation of fairy lights. No one was paying us any attention.

"Come up to my room?" My voice was a husky whisper I barely recognized.

His dark, turbulent eyes widened for a second. Then a slow, sexy smile spread across his face, a look of absolute victory.

"I thought you'd never ask." He captured my hand, his grip possessive. "I need to get you out of here. Now."

We left the warm glow of the fairy lights behind, moving at a pace just shy of a run. He pulled me past the shimmering blue of the resort pool, our footsteps crunching on the shell path that led toward the room blocks. The air was charged with anticipation, humming with tension.

Suddenly, he stopped. In the deep shadow between two sheds, under the heavy scent of a frangipani tree, he spun me around and slammed my back against the rough bark. The impact knocked a sharp gasp from my lungs. His mouth crashed down on mine, a brutal, claiming kiss. This was pure, desperate need. He pressed his body against mine, his shaft a hard, insistent ridge against my stomach, grinding against me in a slow, torturous rhythm that made my knees buckle.

"I've been thinking about this for days," he rasped, his lips brushing mine as he spoke. "I can't stop thinking about you."

"Me, either." I fisted my hands in his shirt, pulling him closer. We kissed again, now fueled by frustration. "So why are we standing here?"

With a grunt, he captured my hand again. His grip was almost painfully tight as he pulled me down the path. The last fifty feet were a blur of urgency, every step charged with the promise of what was coming.

We reached Room 215. I fumbled, the key card slippery in my sweat-slicked hand. Dean was so close behind that I could feel the heat of his chest. His hand closed over mine, gentle then firm, as he slid the card in and shouldered the door open. I stumbled inside.

The room was cool and smelled of fresh flowers. I set my purse on the desk, my heart galloping. When I turned back, Dean was closing the door, the soft click echoing in the silence. He leaned against it, his eyes dark and hungry, then yanked his tie loose with a sharp tug. He pulled it free from his collar and dropped it on the floor, his gaze never leaving mine as he raked a hand through his hair, leaving it wild. There was something desperate in his expression as he stalked toward me, as if he were afraid to blink and miss this.

He reached for my face with both hands, fingers threading into my hair. I rose up and kissed him, mouth open, all the careful rules and fake-dating contracts dissolving under the salt on his lips. He pressed me back against the wall, a picture frame digging into my shoulder. His mouth never left mine, his hands pulling the pins from my hair to let it cascade down my back. Moving down, he gripped my ass, lifting me until my toes skimmed the floor. I gasped into his mouth, and he swallowed it, the sound of my need making him shudder.

He tasted of whiskey and lime, and I couldn't stop myself from nipping his bottom lip. I scraped my nails over his scalp, and he groaned, low and ragged. I wanted to hear that sound again.

He broke the kiss to drag in a shaky breath. "Brynn. I really want you."

I hooked my leg around his and pressed against him. He wasn't lying. "I want you too. So much." I grabbed his shirtfront and yanked him back down, devouring his mouth like I was starved for it.

My whole life I'd played by the rules.

Now I wanted the mess.

I wanted him.

He walked me across the room until my ass hit the wooden desk by the window, sending a stack of resort pamphlets scattering to the floor. I gasped, breathless, and he stepped back to watch me for a second, chest heaving. It was the first time I'd seen him hesitate.

I slowly, deliberately unbuttoned the top of my dress, then leaned back on my elbows against the cool wood. "If you don't get over here, I'm starting without you."

Dean exhaled a sound that was half curse, half groan, and tugged off his shirt in one motion. He was lean and muscled, a faint line of hair trailing from his chest down his stomach. In two strides, he was back at the desk. He braced his hands on either side of my hips and leaned over me, his face just inches from mine.

I bit his earlobe, then slid my tongue down his neck. He shivered, and his control snapped. His hands found the zipper at my side, and in a blur, the dress was gone, replaced by the chill of the room and the heat of his skin.

We tore at each other, every barrier falling away. My bra was gone in a flash. Dean's mouth traced a line from my throat to my shoulder. My hands explored his back, digging into his muscles as he rocked against me. I wanted to memorize every inch of him. His fingers trailed up my thigh, teasing the edge of my panties. I pulled his hand to me, guiding him where I wanted him.

"Dean," I moaned.

A raw, guttural sound tore from his throat. His mouth crashed down on mine again, but his hands were already moving, his fingers hooking into the waistband of my panties. I expected him to slide them down, but there was a sharp tug, the sound of tearing fabric, and then nothing but cool air on my skin. He ripped them away with one hand, the scrap of lace fluttering to the floor, a forgotten casualty.

Before I could even process it, he sank to his knees in front of me, his hands gripping my thighs, thumbs tracing slow, deliberate circles on my inner skin. He lifted my right leg and hooked it over his shoulder before pulling me to the edge of the desk, exposing me completely to his hungry gaze.

Then his mouth was on me. Hot, wet, and perfect.

His tongue swept over my nub, a single, deliberate lick that sent a jolt up my spine, making me gasp his name. He didn't rush. He explored me, his tongue tracing lazy patterns, his lips applying just the right amount of pressure, learning my body with focused intensity. My hips began to buck, one of my hands digging into his hair as I chased the feeling. I braced myself with my other arm as I gasped into the empty night. I was close, so close, the pleasure coiling tight and low in my stomach.

And then he backed off.

He slowed, his tongue becoming achingly gentle, lapping at the edges, denying me the friction I craved. A frustrated whimper escaped my lips, and his wicked laugh filled the air. He dove back in, relentless this time. He devoured me, his tongue a merciless rhythm against me, his fingers digging into the flesh of my ass, holding me in place for the onslaught.

I exploded.

My body convulsed, a scream tearing from my throat as pleasure surged through me. Dean's grip was firm and steady as the aftershocks rocked me. He rode it out, kissing a path up my trembling stomach until he stood, his expression tight with control threatening to snap.

"My turn." A surge of exhilarating power shot through me. I wasn't done. I wanted to see *him* undone.

I pushed him, and he went willingly, letting me spin him until his back was against the wall beside the desk. He was only in his boxer briefs, his erection straining against the thin cotton. I knelt before him, my hands finding the waistband. I hooked my thumbs in and peeled them down his thighs, freeing him. He was thick and hot, and the sight of him, so exposed and waiting for me, was intoxicating.

I took him into my mouth, tasting salt and skin. A ragged groan escaped his throat and vibrated against my lips. I craved more of that sound. His hands tangled in my hair, gripping without pushing, his knuckles white as he held on. I established a steady, deep pace, slowly quickening my rhythm. His hips began to move against my mouth.

"Brynn," he gasped, his voice strained. "Wait. I need to be inside you. Now."

After pulling my head away, he lifted me to my feet. He spun me around and pressed me forward, bending me over the desk. He loomed over me for a second, running his hands over my back before fumbling for his wallet in his pants. He tore a condom wrapper open with his teeth. I watched, mesmerized, as he sheathed himself.

He settled behind me, his hands gripping my hips, and plunged inside from behind, filling me completely. I cried out, a raw sound of pleasure and relief. He was hot and perfect, stretching me, claiming every inch. He moved slowly at first, but that didn't last.

We quickly built to a frantic, sweaty rhythm fueled by desperate need. He slammed into me, again and again, and I met every thrust, my nails digging into the smooth wood of the desk.

I pushed up on my hands, arching my back, and looked over my shoulder at him, my eyes locking with his in the dim light. A low growl rumbled in his chest as he reached around me, his hands closing over my breasts, kneading and squeezing in time with his thrusts. His thumbs found my already hard peaks, rolling them until I cried out again, the pleasure almost too much.

"That's it," he growled, his hips bucking hard against me.

It wasn't enough. I needed more. I grabbed one of his wrists and pulled his hand from my breast. I guided it down, between our slick bodies, pressing his fingers against my center. He found my rhythm, circling and pressing as he drove into me faster, harder.

The pleasure was blinding. I was coming apart, my orgasm building with every slick slide of him inside me and the relentless pressure of his fingers. I felt him tense behind me, his thrusts becoming deeper and more frantic.

"Yes!" I cried out.

I felt the pulse of his release deep inside me at the same moment my climax shattered through me, a wave of white-hot light. I collapsed forward onto the desk, my body shaking, his arms wrapping around me from behind to hold me together. He stayed inside me for a long moment, his forehead resting between my shoulder blades, our rushed, heavy breathing the only sound in the room. Then he withdrew, slowly and deliberately, and turned me around to face him.

His hands came up to frame my face, his thumbs stroking my cheekbones. His eyes were now soft and tender. He didn't speak. He just kissed me in a slow, searching slant of lips that was almost more intimate than what we'd just done.

"Bed," was all he managed to say, his voice a rough whisper against my lips.

He took a step, pulling me with him, but our legs were tangled and unsteady. We stumbled the few feet across the room, a clumsy, breathless mess of limbs, never breaking the kiss, our mouths still fused as we fell in a heap onto the mattress.

He rolled, pulling me tight against him, and gently stroked my hair. It was lulling and hypnotic. The sea washed against the shore, in sync with my heartbeat. The moon hung low in the window, spotlighting the rumpled bed and the mess of clothes on the floor.

Gradually, his hand slowed on my hair, eventually coming to a stop as his breath deepened. I closed my eyes and let myself believe, just for a minute, that this was real. That I could have this. That we could have this. I clung to him, refusing to let go, even as my real life crept back in around the edges.

For one night, I let myself be reckless. I let myself be happy.

Chapter Six

DEAN

I WOKE MID-DREAM. It had been so real—my financial planning place right there on Main Street, with its lampposts and flower baskets. Even in my imagination, it looked like Norman Rockwell had thrown up and created it all.

Yet… I had been so happy. Like a dream had come true.

Awareness crept back in. The silence was different, a deep, unfamiliar quiet, punctuated only by the low whirr of an air conditioner. My throat was dry, my limbs heavy. Sated. I cracked an eye open. The morning light was a pale, hazy blue, filtered through thin curtains. A woman's arm was slung over my waist, her breathing a soft, steady rhythm against my back.

Panic bloomed within me, sour and icy cold. I wasn't in my bed.

I was in Brynn Vance's.

It was supposed to be fake. A vacation charade easily erased and forgotten. Instead, I was drowning in the proof

—her warm, sleeping body pressed against mine. Her bare thighs against mine. The fact that we were both naked under the covers, and it wasn't even 8:00 a.m.

I sat bolt upright, peeling away from her cling. The sheet dropped from my chest and hips, exposing every inch of me to the prying gaze of the morning. I barely noticed. My heart pounded, my hands already clammy with sweat.

Last night, it was a den of possibility and euphoria. Now, it was a map leading somewhere I never intended to go. Our clothes were everywhere. Her bra hung off the chair. A framed photo of her and Holly sat on the nightstand—something she'd obviously brought with her. A beach towel in a blinding shade of turquoise hung on a wall hook. Every object was a landmark leading to a place I had spent years avoiding.

It was all so goddamn domestic. So feminine and welcoming. I wanted to crawl out of my own body. I swung my legs off the bed and planted my feet on the cool tile, but my chest cinched tighter with every breath.

That's when she stirred. Behind me, the sheets rustled, and the weight of her gaze on my back was a physical thing. I tensed, pretending not to notice. Maybe if I stayed still, she'd go back to sleep.

"Dean?" Her voice was hoarse, half-asleep, but soft. "Hey. What's wrong?"

I gripped the mattress so hard my knuckles went white. "Nothing. Just need some air."

The lie hung between us, paper-thin. She sat up, dragging the covers with her, wrapping herself in cotton and concern.

"You okay?" she repeated, quieter this time.

The concern in her voice triggered something primal and embarrassing. I felt it in the roots of my teeth, the base of my spine. I'd spent years training myself to be self-contained, invulnerable, the kind of man who could walk away from anything. From anyone. But now, with Brynn in my head, on my body, everywhere—my training failed.

She reached out and touched my shoulder. I jerked away like she'd pressed a lit cigarette to my skin. My breath whistled in and out as fast as a dog panting. But I couldn't get enough air.

"Dean, please talk to me."

I couldn't. My pulse spiked, my vision got hazy at the edges. If I opened my mouth, something ugly would come out. She slid closer, careful and slow, until her bare knee touched my thigh. Her hand hovered near my arm, not quite touching this time.

"You're having a panic attack." There was no judgment in her voice. Just a gentle fact, as if she were explaining something to her first graders.

And that only made me feel more inadequate. I braced my elbows on my knees and tried to breathe. "Not… not a panic attack."

She exhaled, not quite a snort or a laugh. "Okay. Just regular hyperventilating, then."

Her words should have pissed me off, but they were gentler than I deserved.

I focused on a spot on the floor, where the tile was cracked in the shape of a Y. "I need to get out of here."

She didn't move, didn't pull back. "You can leave, but it won't help. I know how this works."

I almost laughed, but the sound snagged in my chest. "Doubt it."

She waited, giving me time to climb back into myself. When I didn't speak, she nudged, just enough to tip me over. "Just breathe, Dean. It's okay. Tell me what's happening."

"I had a fiancée," I said. The words came out cracked,

foreign. I couldn't believe I was telling her. "Three years ago. Thought she was the one. We were engaged a year and a half. I moved for her, changed my job, the whole nine yards."

Brynn sat motionless, listening.

"I turned down two promotions because she didn't want me traveling. We were supposed to get married in Asheville in October. Peak leaf season."

I realized my hands were shaking and knotted them together.

"She left me a month before the wedding. For a guy she met at some spin class. Said she was sick of being the only person in the relationship willing to take a risk. Said I was a doormat."

I tried to laugh, but it sounded strangled. "I spent a week drinking vodka in a Holiday Inn. Then I packed up and moved to Atlanta, took the best job I could get. I was determined to become so successful, so untouchable, that no one would ever dare call me a doormat again. Didn't talk to my parents for six months. Ghosted all my social media."

Brynn made a small, sympathetic noise, but she let me keep going.

"It's not like I haven't been with anyone since then," I said, the words rushing out now, a desperate attempt to explain something I didn't understand myself. "But it was always on my terms. My rules. It was safe.

"This… panic thing has never happened before. I don't… I can't." My voice broke. I gestured vaguely at the room, at the rumpled sheets between us, at her. Then I dropped my head into my hands, humiliated by my loss of control. "I'm not a relationship guy, Brynn. Do you understand? I don't do this. I don't let people in. Not anymore."

Brynn didn't say anything, just scooted closer and rested her hand—warm, steady—over mine.

My first instinct was to pull away, but the heat of her skin anchored me. I stared at our joined hands, my own trembling, hers calm. I couldn't figure out whether to flip my hand over and lace our fingers together or bolt straight out of the room.

She squeezed once, then let go, preventing me from having to decide. "Thank you for telling me."

I had no idea what to do with that. All I could think was how pathetic I sounded, how Brynn deserved someone better, someone who wouldn't freak out just because her life was more real than a bank statement.

She didn't try to fix it. She just sat with me, our bodies still, the only sound the distant hush of waves on the beach.

For the first time in years, I let myself feel it. The grief, the shame, the hollowed-out space that loss leaves behind. It was awful, and it was a relief. The human heart wasn't meant for this kind of exposure. I could handle being naked, but being known? That was a different animal— one that clawed its way up my ribcage as soon as the silence stretched a little too long.

My hand trembled. It still felt warm where Brynn had touched it. The vulnerability in the room calcified, transforming into something sharp and hostile. Every second she didn't run for the hills, my internal alarm shrieked louder.

I needed a reset, a hard break, anything to cut through this gluey aftermath. I vaulted to my feet. The room spun for a second, then snapped into perfect, judgmental clarity.

"Shit, sorry," I said, already regretting the way my voice sounded—raw, frayed, as if I'd chewed glass in my sleep.

Brynn's gaze flickered. "Dean, it's okay. Really."

She meant it. That was the problem. The more compassion she showed me, the more I wanted to set myself on fire. I paced a tight, nervous loop from the bed to the tiny closet, picking up clothes as I went. The room felt smaller with every step I took, like it was designed to compress me into a manageable size.

I snatched my boxer briefs from the foot of the bed and stepped into them with such force I almost lost my balance. My shirt came next, wrinkled and damp, still carrying the scent of her skin and cheap detergent. I yanked it over my head, struggling with the collar like I was wrestling a python.

Brynn sat up, arms wrapped around her knees, the sheet draped carelessly across her chest. Her hair was a mess, and her cheeks were blotched with pillow marks. The urge to look at her was overpowering. I didn't.

"Dean, has it occurred to you that maybe you're reacting this way because what's happened between us is different than your usual flings? That it means something?"

I finally met her eyes, just for a second. It was a mistake. She looked exposed, still worried for me, even now. I darted my gaze away as the tendrils coiled in my stomach again and knotted up.

No! I just got it all under control again. End this now. Get out while you still can.

"No. What happened last night was fun." My words tumbled out in a snarl. "But let's not pretend this is more than a vacation fling."

She flinched like I'd thrown something, but I couldn't stop. I needed to get ahead of the next blow, the one I could feel winding up inside her.

"I mean, come on." I gestured vaguely at the window, where the morning sun lit up the marina and the cheerful pastel houses. "People don't come to places like this to find themselves. They come to forget. That's the whole point."

Brynn's eyes narrowed. "Is that what you're doing? Forgetting?"

I barked a laugh, hollow. "Trying to. It's not working, though. Goddammit, this whole thing was *fake!*"

She watched me with wide, stricken eyes. The crushed look on her face should have made me feel powerful. It didn't. It made me want to crawl under the bed and wait for the world to end.

I kept talking, because it was the only way to drown out the sound of my own heart. "I'm not built for this, Brynn. The mornings after. I have a life in Atlanta—a good one. I'm going to get back on a plane, and this place will just be a story I'll tell at a bar sometime. If I even bother."

She sat up straighter. "That's bullshit, and you know it."

"Maybe." I shrugged, finding my pants on the floor and pulling them on as fast as I could. "But it's easier than pretending this is something it's not."

She shook her head, incredulous. "You just poured your heart out to me, Dean. Probably for the first time ever. You think I didn't hear that?"

I tried to smile, but my lips wouldn't cooperate. "I'm just trying to do you a favor, Vance. You don't want a guy like me."

She stared, her expression inscrutable. "I think I get to decide what I want."

"Yeah, well, that's your mistake." My words landed flat, each one a pebble in a dry well. "But I'm not going to let you make it."

I couldn't stand the weight of her eyes anymore. I turned my back, zipped my pants, and grabbed my shoes.

The urge to bolt was so strong I could feel the adrenaline in my toes.

She didn't chase me.

I stood, staring at the closed door, my breath shallow and fast. My skin crawled. In the reflection of the window, I looked like a man who'd just lost a fight he didn't know he was in.

For a second, I thought about turning around and trying again. But the words wouldn't come. Instead, I slipped my shoes on, not bothering with socks, and yanked open the door.

The last thing I heard was Brynn's voice behind me, "Coward."

She wasn't wrong. Wasn't that the story of my life?

I left the room, every muscle vibrating, counting down the hours until my flight. There were too many. I needed to get on an earlier one. Every step away from Brynn felt like the last, desperate gasp of a drowning man.

I made it ten paces down the hall before her voice rang out, clear and sharp as broken glass. "Dean Mercer, if you take one more step, you'll regret it."

I stopped, the pulse throbbing behind my eyes. I could have kept going. Should have. But the promise in her voice wasn't a threat—it was a dare. So I turned.

Brynn stood in the doorway, wrapped in nothing but a bedsheet and righteous fury. Her hair was a wild tangle, her cheeks blotched with anger. She looked stronger than I'd ever seen her. A hell of a lot stronger than me.

She clutched the sheet in one fist. "God, you really are scared. Go ahead and run, then. But at least admit it to yourself. You're leaving because this was real, not because it was fake."

My mouth became a parched desert. "Brynn—"

"No. You don't get to say my name. You don't get to

have the last word." She pointed down the hall, her arm shaking. "Go back to your real life. Forget this ever happened." She stepped back into her room and slammed the door.

I walked, shoes untied, shirt still wrinkled, the skin on my back tingling with loss. Tingling with the memory of last night. I made it to the end of the corridor before I stopped and pressed my forehead to the cool plaster wall. I didn't cry.

But I wanted to.

I kept moving, hoping the ache would ease with distance and knowing it wouldn't. Knowing I'd just blown the best thing to happen to me in a long time. The image of that business on Main Street flashed one last time in my mind before I ruthlessly shoved it down and locked it away.

Chapter Seven

BRYNN

PACKING a suitcase should be a ten-minute job. Roll, fold, stack, zip. But I'd spent the last hour staging a small-scale invasion of my closet, every shirt and sock. The contents of my life—wrinkled sundresses, half-used travel bottles, an embarrassing amount of hair products—looked both pitifully meager and overwhelming.

I yanked on a buckle inside, but it jammed. The resistance sent a spike of rage up my neck. I wanted to hurl the whole thing off the balcony. Instead, I slumped onto the mattress and stared at the ceiling fan. My jaw ached from being clenched so long. Every time I swallowed, my throat fought back, the memory of Dean's exit still snagged there like a fishhook. He'd been gone a couple of hours, and I'd immediately latched onto the mindless activity of packing to delay the inevitable.

It was almost funny how heartbreak turned you into your worst self. Last night, I'd been full of heat and daring. Today, I was a stone statue—heavy, silent, hollow. The crying hadn't started yet, but I could feel it lurking, waiting for me to loosen my grip. Outside my window, gulls shrieked, utterly unbothered by human drama. I envied them.

I rolled a shirt, my hands shaking enough to make the seams crooked. I started over, desperate to get it right. It was the only thing I could control. I held up the blue linen dress, the one I'd worn to the mixer the first night. It seemed so long ago.

The *moving on with my life* dress.

I held it up to my face, the fabric cool against my cheek. "Where am I going to wear it? To grade papers on my couch? To another awkward faculty mixer? To a solo dinner at the same Thai place I always go to?"

My gaze dropped to the other items in my suitcase—sensible shorts, my one swimsuit, my teacher-friendly tops. I tried to picture myself putting them back in my closet in Atlanta, slotting them back into the neat, predictable, safe life I'd built.

The thought brought a wave of suffocating dread.

I clenched my eyes and said the truth out loud. "My safe life in Atlanta isn't a home. It's a waiting room. I've been waiting for my real life to start for years, and I'm scared it just walked out the door."

The idea of going back to that quiet, empty apartment, to that life where I had a great job but nothing else ever happened, was more terrifying than the prospect of staying here with a broken heart. But would working here as a teacher be any different? The more I thought about it, the more unrealistic Doris's off-the-cuff idea of selling me the ice cream shop seemed. I'd never qualify for financing.

I couldn't go forward. I didn't want to go back. But what else was there? I rolled up the dress and placed it inside the duffel.

A soft knock came at the door. I knew it was Holly before she spoke—nobody else in the family knocked gently. "Brynn? You up?"

I almost lied. Said I was fine or pretended to be sleeping. She was probably here to gush about her post-wedding-night bliss, and I wasn't sure I could take it. But the shape of her shadow under the door broke my will.

"Yeah," I replied and opened the door. "Come in."

Holly slipped in, her hair in a messy bun that defied the laws of physics. She took in the battlefield of clothes, her gaze flicking from my scattered, half-packed clothing to my empty stare. "Did a hurricane come through? Or is this some sort of metaphor?"

"Packing," I said. My voice was as flat as a test pattern.

She hovered by the desk, clearly wanting to hug me but too smart to close in before I was ready. "You're not leaving until tomorrow."

"I wanted to get a head start."

She sat on the foot of the bed, careful not to disturb the shirts. "B, are you okay?"

I let out a sound, something between a cough and a laugh. "Not exactly."

Holly chewed her lip, then picked up a T-shirt and started folding. I stared at the angry red half-moons where my nails had dug into my palms. The words were a clot in my chest, but I forced them out.

"He left," I said, flopping onto the unmade bed. The one that still smelled like him. "Dean, I mean. He just… left."

She blinked, her expression shifting from concern to confusion. "Left? What do you mean, left? I thought the plan was to fake it through the trip."

I shook my head, heat pricking behind my eyes. "That *was* the plan. But it… it stopped being fake for me, Hols." I snapped my jaw shut, embarrassed by the tears worming out despite all my defenses.

Holly edged closer and sat, her hand finding my ankle. "Brynn, what happened?"

I tried to smile and failed. "It stopped being a joke. I fell for him, and we had this stupid, amazing night. It became real to me. And I thought he felt it too."

"And?"

I thought of his raw, very real panic attack. No, I wouldn't talk about that. Regardless of what happened, that was a confidence between him and me. "He woke up and looked at me like I'd ruined his life. He couldn't even stay in the same room. He's probably already rescheduled his flight and is on his way to the airport."

"Oh, honey." Holly's expression was pained. "I saw it too. The way he looked at you during the toasts, the dancing… that wasn't an act. I'm so sorry."

Her thumb made slow circles on my foot. The touch was an anchor in my storm. I pressed the heel of my hand to my eye, trying to stop the flood. "He called it a vacation fling. Said people come here to forget, not to find themselves." I tried to laugh, but it came out as a shudder. "He made it sound like I was the only idiot who didn't get the memo."

The ache in my chest just got sharper, a splinter working its way deeper every time I drew breath. "I'm done, Hols. I'm done letting my happiness depend on a man who runs the second things get complicated."

Holly's eyes were red-rimmed now too. "You don't have to decide anything right now. You're allowed to hurt first."

I nodded, but the resolve in me was already hardening, like a scar forming over fresh skin.

"What about staying here to teach?"

I'd told her about Eli's suggestion, but not about Doris's offer. Now that seemed more like a blessing. "I need to leave. I can't stay here, not with everyone watching and waiting for me to fall apart."

She reached for my hand. "You're not falling apart. You're making a decision."

"I'm making the only one I know how to. I'm going back to Atlanta."

After squeezing my fingers, she placed some toiletries in a zip-close bag. "When do you fly out again?"

"Tomorrow afternoon. I'll Uber to the airport."

"Not happening. I'll take you. And I'm bringing donuts."

A strangled laugh escaped me. Holly grinned, the same lopsided smile she'd worn since we were kids. She piled the bag into my suitcase. "Anything else you want to pack?"

"Just my dignity. Assuming I can find it."

She shook her head. "You never lost it. That's the problem with you, B. You're too good at holding it together. It makes people like Dean think you don't need them."

I wanted to argue, but it was too close to the truth. "I really thought he was different. I thought he saw me."

Holly's smile was gentle but fierce. "He did, and it scared the hell out of him. That's not your fault."

I wiped my nose on my T-shirt sleeve. "So what now?"

She zipped the bag with authority. "Now we get coffee —Irish coffee!—and go to the beach. Say mean things about men until you feel better."

The thought of sunshine and caffeine was almost enough to make the world seem survivable, but I couldn't do that to her. "That's a wonderful idea for me. You have a wonderful new husband waiting for you, and I'm sure you didn't come here to hear my mega pity party."

"You've heard mine often enough. We've been through a lot together."

I hugged her tightly. "We sure have. But now you have a new shoulder to lean on. Go. I'll be fine. Really."

"Love you, B."

"Right back at you, Hols."

I got to Tidal Hops right after it opened for lunch service. It was too hot for Irish coffee, so Braden Coleridge made me an iced one without blinking an eye. I only wallowed on the beach for a short while before I pulled myself out of it. I owed Doris a goodbye. If I was going to leave Dove Key, I wanted to at least say goodbye to the only place that had ever felt like mine.

After a thorough shower to wash Dean completely out of my life, I strolled down Main Street. The flower baskets swayed in the gentle breeze, filling the air with their perfume. The humidity clung to my skin, a reminder of the weight I'd carried here and the heavier load I'd be hauling home.

The Corner Scoop sat at the corner of Main and Harbor, painted the color of lavender and old driftwood. The bell over the door chimed, and the blast of frigid AC hit me like a small miracle. Inside, the shop was empty except for a father bribing his toddler with sprinkles, and Doris behind the counter.

She caught sight of me, and her face broke into a smile that could stop traffic. "Well, if it isn't the return of the prodigal scooper!"

I tried to smile, but my face barely cooperated. "Hi, Doris. Didn't want to leave without saying goodbye."

She enveloped me in a hug that threatened to suffocate me. It felt wonderful. "You always were a considerate one." When she let go, she kept a grip on my shoulders, giving me the once-over. Her eyes searched my face, picking up on every fracture line. "You look like you've seen a ghost."

"Rough visit," I said.

She arched an eyebrow and jerked her chin toward the back. "C'mon. Sit. I'll get us coffee after I shoo out those two customers and lock the door."

The back room was just as I remembered—folding chairs, a battered card table, walls lined with snapshots of every teenager who'd survived a shift. I sat, the old vinyl squeaking beneath me. Doris reappeared with two mugs of coffee, strong and dark as engine oil. No whiskey in them, either. "Want to talk about it?" The silence stretched until she sighed. "Let me guess. It's a guy."

I choked. "Isn't it always?"

"Only for the ones worth the trouble."

I stared into my mug, inhaling the steam. "I thought we had something, and he just… walked out. Now I don't know what to do."

Doris nodded, unsurprised. "Men can be like ice cream on a hot day. Sweet, then gone before you blink." She laid a heavy, calloused hand over mine. "You don't need to leave, Brynn. This island's big enough for a broken heart and a comeback."

I squeezed her hand. "I don't think I can. We were together less than a week! How can every corner, every breath of bracing air, remind me of him? Remind me that I'm here alone?"

"That's not a reason to run. That's a reason to fight for what you want." Doris inhaled and leveled a sharp glance at me. "A chain out of Tampa made an offer on the Scoop yesterday. A good one. I told them I'd think about it."

The words landed like a punch. "Really?"

"I hate the idea of selling to a chain. But I'm tired, Brynn. After our talk…" She leaned in. "Are you sure you don't want to buy the shop? Because if you do, I need to know today."

The room spun. "I can't, Doris! I'm a teacher. I don't know anything about running a business."

She barked a laugh. "Bullshit. You ran this shop for two months that summer when my knee gave out. You know more than most."

I shook my head, the excuses sounding weak, even to me. "I've never owned anything. What if I fail?"

What if Rob was right? What if I am utterly unambitious and this is just a fantasy?

Doris squeezed my hand so hard my knuckles blanched. "So what? Life's not about getting it right on the first try. Sometimes you have to say yes, even if it scares you."

The silence that followed was heavier, but also brighter. I looked around the little shop—the photographs, the ancient espresso machine, the rainbow of scoops. I thought about what it would mean to have this, to belong, to stay. My heart twisted.

"I'll think about it," I whispered.

Doris nodded, satisfied. "Good. You've got until close of business. But if you walk away, you'll always wonder."

She stood and returned to her routine as if the fate of the Scoop and my life weren't hanging in the balance. I stayed in that chair a long time, listening to the thumping whirr of the ancient AC. The question wasn't whether I wanted the Scoop. The question was whether I was brave enough to want anything at all.

I stared at my reflection in the bottom of the coffee cup and tried to imagine a future where I didn't run away. It looked better than I expected.

After a while, Doris reappeared in the doorway. "You're still here, huh?"

I rested my head in my hands. "Okay, I'll admit it. I love the idea of owning this place. It's home to me in a way Atlanta has never been. But, Doris, I'm a school teacher! I've been responsible with my money, but I don't have a trust fund, you know. How could it possibly work?"

She nodded sagely. "Give me ten minutes. I'll be back."

I blinked at the empty doorway. What could she be up to?

True to her word, Doris was soon back in the Scoop's back room, car keys in one hand.

"Let's go," she barked.

"Huh? Go where?"

"As you rightly pointed out, we need some counsel. So we're off to the bank. Come on, girl. Time's a-wastin'."

She flipped the sign to *Closed* before relocking the door behind us. The air on Main Street shimmered over the pavement as we marched down the sidewalk. Doris set a pace that bordered on a power walk, and I trailed behind, my heart thudding.

We rounded the corner to the Dove Key Community Credit Union. Doris marched right over to a corner office, where a middle-aged Hispanic woman in a smart business suit, her salt-and-pepper hair pulled into a sleek ponytail, sized us up. "Afternoon, Doris. This the one you mentioned?"

Doris patted my back. "Yep. This is Brynn Vance. Brynn, this is the small business loan officer, Gloria Suarez."

After we shook hands, Gloria smiled and motioned us to sit at a table inside her glass-walled office. "I can get you some coffee. Cream and sugar, or just nerves?"

"Just nerves," I said with a laugh. Then I pointed at my T-shirt and shorts. "No thanks. I would have dressed more appropriately if I'd known we were coming here."

"Nonsense," Doris added. "When something's right, appearances don't matter."

Gloria shut the door and sat across from us. "I'm familiar with Doris's books. She runs a great business, but transition is always tricky. The first step isn't a mountain of paperwork—it's a handshake on paper. It's called a Letter of Intent." She pulled out a folder. "It says you're formally expressing your interest in buying the Corner Scoop based on the outlined terms. It allows me to start the official loan underwriting and tells Doris she can take the property off the market while we work out the details. It's the first step." She laid out a few sheets outlining the seller-financing terms Doris proposed over the phone.

Doris was willing to carry the loan. For me. I swallowed hard over the lump in my throat.

"It's a good deal, Brynn," Gloria continued. "Since it's seller-financed, Doris will be your partner for the first few years. She'll retain a minority stake in the business until the initial loan is paid down. That means she has skin in the game, which the bank loves to see. On top of that, she's agreed to stay on as an advisor through the first summer to make sure you land on your feet. This is Dove Key. We look out for our own."

I glanced at Doris, my mouth hanging open. A partner? This was more than just a sale. She was offering me a safety net woven from her own legacy. "Doris! I can't believe this. Are you sure?"

She responded with a wink, as if it were the most natural thing in the world. "This is the right move. I feel it in my achy old bones, honey."

Turning back to the paper, I tried to process the numbers, but my fears were louder. "I don't even know if I'd be approved for a loan."

"Well, let's find out," Gloria said with a practical smile.

"With your permission, I can run a preliminary credit check right now. It'll give us a good idea of where you stand."

I nodded, my heart knocking against my ribs as I handed over my driver's license. Gloria tapped on her keyboard for a moment. Her printer whirred. She examined the report, and her professional smile became genuine.

"Well, Brynn," Gloria said, turning the paper so I could see. "You have an excellent credit score. Clean history, low debt-to-income. From the bank's perspective, you're a very solid bet."

Doris leaned back, satisfied. "Told you it's doable."

The validation was a balm on my frayed nerves. My entire future balanced on the edge of this moment.

Gloria pushed a single-page document toward me. "It's just the Letter of Intent for now. If you sign, we start the process. You can walk away any time before closing. But this is you telling us—and yourself—that you're serious."

I stared at the fancy bank pen, the urge to run warring with the urge to reach for my dream.

Doris caught my eye. "You said you wanted something different, kid. This is it. And I'd never hang you out to dry. I've got your back, girl."

My hands were sweating. I wiped them on my shorts and picked up the pen. The tip hovered over the signature line. I thought about Atlanta, about the empty apartments and safe choices that had stopped being fulfilling long ago. Then I thought about seventeen-year-old me, scraping gum off tabletops for minimum wage and loving every second.

I pressed the pen to the paper and signed. My signature was a bit of a disaster—crooked, letters running together—but it was there.

My name, on the line.

When I set the pen down, Doris's hand found my shoulder. "Atta girl."

Gloria stood, beaming. "Congratulations, Brynn. You're about to have an unforgettable summer."

Outside, the sun shined with more promise and fewer UV rays. Main Street looked different—not smaller, but more possible. More *mine*.

When we returned to the Corner Scoop, Doris insisted we celebrate. "Only a banana split will do."

She made us each a triple scoop and insisted we eat it on the porch, the world's messiest victory lap. My heart still twisted at the memory of Dean. At what had started here but had never had a chance to blossom. In the end, I'd been willing to fight for what I wanted. If he couldn't do the same, dammit, he didn't deserve me.

As I licked a streak of chocolate ice cream from the spoon, I watched small-town life go by. Kids rode bikes, a dog stole fries at a café across the street, a couple argued in lazy, affectionate tones.

And my life clicked into place.

At last, I wasn't settling and calling it safety. I was reaching toward a dream, and it was sweet as hell.

Chapter Eight

DEAN

I USED to think morning sunlight was energizing—one of those *rise and grind* platitudes that made sleep feel like a personal failing. In Atlanta, the sun came up hard, refracting through a mile of glass and steel before it hit my apartment. My apartment was an open-concept box, dressed in grayscale and chrome. My furniture looked like it had been ordered in a single, hurried click. Which it had. The only decorations were a set of black-and-white prints and a potted succulent that had been dead for months.

It was day twenty-six since I'd left Dove Key, and my desk was stacked with market projections I couldn't bring myself to care about. My focus was shot. I kept unlocking my phone, my thumb hovering over the Main Street real estate listings I kept telling myself I wasn't interested in.

As if to punish myself, I tapped to bring up the hopeless text conversations that had started three days after I got back to Atlanta, and the reality of what I'd done—what I'd lost—hit me. The texts where I tried to tell Brynn

I'd been an idiot, and she agreed before telling me to go to hell. Not quite that bluntly, though that was what I deserved. At first, she'd been more polite, informing me she was buying the Corner Scoop and relocating to Dove Key. That text hit me with the force of a sledgehammer.

She was slipping away from me.

I didn't delete any of the texts. The words were burned into my memory, but I read them again anyway. The last exchange was from a week ago.

Dean: Hey. How are you? I panicked. I'm not proud, but I am sorry.

THE THREE LITTLE dots appeared and disappeared for an eternity before her reply finally landed hours later. A clean, polite kill shot.

Brynn: I appreciate that, but you made your feelings clear, and we live very different lives, right? I'm a small-town girl and you're the big-city man. I wish you the best, but there's no reason for us to keep in touch. Let's move on.

I TRIED ONE MORE TIME. A desperate, stupid Hail Mary.

Dean: I'm sorry again. I'm here if you want to talk.

. . .

AND NEXT TO MY TEXT—READ. 8:14 p.m.

No reply since.

I locked the screen and tossed the phone onto the couch. *I wish you the best* was the corporate-speak of breakups, a polite dismissal that stung more than anger ever could. She hadn't just shut the door. She'd locked it, bolted it, and walked away. And I was the one who'd handed her the goddamn key.

The air was thick with the distant hum of downtown. When I first moved here, that noise felt like promise. Now it just sounded like a million people shouting into a void. My second cup of coffee tasted like scorched earth, and my hands shook just enough to make typing a challenge. I blamed it on the caffeine, but the real problem was I hadn't slept more than three hours a night since that last text.

I tried to focus on the quarterly projections, but my brain kept drifting to images of Brynn's face as she told me off, the sound of her voice when she called me a coward. I hated that she was right. I hated even more that I missed her so much.

I ran my hands through my hair—longer than I liked —and gave the screen a withering look. I set the mug down so hard it sloshed onto a stack of old conference badges. I didn't bother to wipe it up.

The phone rang again. Josh's name lit up, just as it had the last three mornings. I'd let him go to voicemail every time. This time, knowing what he was probably calling about, I answered just to get it over with.

"Mercer," I said, my voice sharp.

"Don't hang up," Josh said. "I'm not calling to talk about my newlywed happiness, okay? I'm calling because

Holly is worried about Brynn. And I'm worried about you."

"Nothing's wrong. Stop worrying." I let the silence stretch.

Instead of filling it with platitudes, he said, "You sound like hell, man. What happened in Dove Key? Holly told me about the fake-to-real thing that happened with you two. But why did you bolt and disappear off the face of the earth?"

My first instinct was to laugh it off. Second was to lie. Third—because I was out of defenses—was to just stand there, my own emptiness echoing back through the line.

"I'm fine," I said finally.

Josh didn't buy it. "We're not sure Brynn is. Did you know she moved to Dove Key last week?"

"I know." A cold wash of shame hit me. "But that's not my problem."

Josh didn't miss a beat. "Look, I don't know what went down, and maybe it's none of my business. But Holly says Brynn admitted she misses you. And you sound like someone's holding your head underwater."

Josh was the guy who listened, who let you vent, then said the one thing that made you think maybe it wasn't all pointless. He waited, giving me time. I stared out at the city view that stretched to the horizon, everything measured, perfect, and meaningless.

"I blew it." My words tasted raw, like gravel. "She got close, and I freaked out. I said some things. Not good things."

Josh exhaled. "You want to talk about it?"

I stopped in front of the window, my forehead almost touching the glass. The city vibrated below, but all I heard was the echo of my own voice. "I didn't mean to hurt her. That wasn't the plan."

"Nobody ever means to, Dean. That's the problem."

I shut my eyes and pinched the bridge of my nose. I could see Brynn's face, every flicker of hurt, every flash of hope. I could still feel every inch of her body, taste every moment of her sweetness. I could see her inside that ice cream shop in Dove Key, sunlight in her hair, looking like a future I never thought I wanted and was now terrified to lose.

"It was the morning after," I said, each word pulled out like a splinter. "I woke up and everything felt—too close. Too real. And I said things I can't take back."

"Like what?"

"I told her it was just a fling. Fake. That it didn't matter. She didn't. That I didn't want more." My voice cracked, an ugly sound in the empty room. "I made her believe it was all a game. I didn't mean any of it. I just... I didn't know what else to do."

Josh was silent for a beat. "Why'd you do it?"

I turned from the window and scanned the room. The pristine kitchen with a knife block still in its shrink-wrap. The living room with its single shelf of finance and leadership tomes. The espresso machine I'd never figured out how to use.

"She got to me," I said, hating how weak it sounded. "In just a few days, she got inside my heart. I don't know how to be a real thing anymore. I thought if I pushed her away first, it would hurt less."

Josh gave a little snort. "How's that working out for you?"

I almost smiled. "Like a charm, asshole."

He let me stew in it. "You know, I never told you this, but Holly almost dumped me after our first semester. She said that I was so busy avoiding mistakes I never actually showed up for my own life."

I pictured Josh, steady and even-tempered. Happily married. The idea that he'd ever lost his footing was comforting.

"You ever think about your ex?" he asked, so abrupt it cut right through me.

"Jesus, not if I can help it."

He didn't laugh or snort. I could picture him sitting there, dead serious. "She called you a doormat. Said you were too easy to please. And your answer was to build a whole new life to prove her wrong."

I bristled, but Josh kept going, his voice quiet but relentless. "You got the high-profile Atlanta job. The apartment. You made yourself untouchable. You kept everyone at arm's length because if nobody gets in, nobody can walk away."

I looked at my hand. It was trembling. I clenched it into a fist, but it didn't help.

"You ever ask yourself what you really want?" Josh asked. "Or have you just been reacting to what you don't?"

I stared at the expensive apartment, utterly devoid of personality. "I don't know."

It was the most honest thing I'd managed since I left Dove Key.

"Maybe start there." Josh's voice was softer now. "You're still letting your ex control your life, Dean. You're not your job or your apartment. The only person making those rules is *you*. You don't have to prove a thing to anyone, including yourself. So call an audible—change the play. Stop running from something—Brynn—that might change your life."

I nodded, though he couldn't see it. The anger had drained out of me, replaced by a dull ache. I walked to the fridge, opened it, and stared at a single can of seltzer. It seemed symbolic. "Maybe I needed to hear that."

"It's true," Josh replied. "Call her. Email her. Hell, text her if nothing else. Otherwise, this will eat you alive, man."

"Thanks for listening, Josh. I'm sorry I unloaded on all your newlywed bliss."

A tiny smile lifted one side of my mouth at his laugh. "Yeah, well, you're an asshole, right? Let me know how it goes. We're worried about you two."

"I will." I ended the call and tossed my phone absently in my hand.

The next text I got was a news alert about a jump in shipping futures, which would've thrilled me a month ago. Now it just felt like someone else's life. I scrolled to Brynn's contact, hovered over her name, then set the phone down. I needed a minute.

I walked through the apartment, pacing tight circles. I thought about the dive shop, about the way the air in Dove Key felt thick and *real*. I thought about Brynn's laugh, the stubborn set of her jaw, the way she'd looked at me like she could see every one of my worst impulses. And might learn to love me anyway. Until I tossed it all away.

I didn't deserve her. But I wasn't going to let that stop me this time.

I sat at my desk, opened a new draft email, and started typing.

Brynn,

I owe you a lot of apologies. I know I hurt you. I ran because I was scared, not because I didn't care. The truth is, I've never cared more about anything in my life. I want to do better. I want to try.

—Dean

. . .

I STARED at the words until they blurred, my finger hovering over the send button, a single click away from… what? More waiting? Staring at my phone, hoping for a reply that might never come, putting the ball in her court after *I* was the one who walked off the field?

It was the coward's way out. An apology lobbed from the safety of a thousand miles away.

Words were what I'd used to wound her—sharp, easy, and disposable.

Vacation fling. Just a charade.

How could more words, typed on a screen, ever fix that? They couldn't. This wasn't a negotiation to be handled over email. This was a mess I had to stand in the middle of. An email asked for forgiveness.

Showing up earned it.

My jaw set. I highlighted the entire draft, every raw and honest word, and hit delete. I watched the confession vanish. The screen was blank, but my mind was clear. From my living room, the view was perfect—downtown Atlanta on display, every luxury car crawling through intersections, every sidewalk pulsing with ambition. It had once felt like an achievement, a trophy. Now it just looked like a high-rise zoo, the glass a reminder of how easy it is to build a cage and convince yourself it was a throne.

I leaned back and tipped my head toward the ceiling. That image flooded my mind again. The storefront with my name on it. The flower baskets. A street that was the heart of a town. I picked up my phone again and scrolled to the listings I had bookmarked. My favorite was still active. My heart hummed, but not with panic. More like adrenaline. A kind of relief, like stepping out of a packed elevator onto an open rooftop.

A decision made.

I thought of Brynn. Her unfiltered laugh that dared me to stop pretending. Her stubborn optimism. How the taste of her lips was the first thing I'd wanted more of in years. I wanted that life. The messy, loud, embarrassing one, where people knew you well enough to see you screw up and loved you anyway.

If Brynn was going to run toward something, the least I could do was show up at the starting line.

I cracked my knuckles and opened a new email window. The subject line was *Resignation*. I wrote quickly.

To Whom It May Concern:

Effective two weeks from today, I am stepping down from my role and leaving the company. Thank you for the opportunity, but I've realized what I need most can't be found in a spreadsheet.

All the best,
Dean Mercer

I READ IT OVER. No deletes. No regrets. I hovered over the *Send* button, savoring the feeling of risk—of freedom. Then I sent it.

I pulled up a travel site and searched for a flight to Key West. There were two options. I picked one that left in three hours, paid extra for an aisle seat, and sent the boarding pass to my phone. I reserved a car, and then I was ready.

I examined my apartment. I'd packed it with statement

pieces but never invited anyone to see them. I'd paid a premium for the view but never actually looked at it. It was time to go.

I pulled a duffel from the hall closet and tossed in a stack of clothes and a battered paperback I'd never finished. I closed the door behind me, the latch clicking like a starter's pistol. The elevator was empty, the descent smooth and fast.

I walked out into the night, the Atlanta air thick with humidity and promise. I took a cab to the airport, watching the skyline recede in the rearview. Somewhere between Peachtree and the terminal, I realized I was smiling.

Chapter Nine

BRYNN

I QUICKLY DISCOVERED there was a world of difference between working in an ice cream shop and owning one. Well, almost owning one. I was waiting on pins and needles for the final loan approval. I knew the muscle memory of it —the flick of the wrist for the perfect scoop, the constant war with rainbow sprinkles—but the sense of it was entirely new. Now, I got to walk into a place every morning that smelled like hope, birthday cake, and *mine*.

I wore the evidence of it all on my apron, which looked less retro soda fountain and more like I'd lost a food fight with a unicorn. But this was my place now. My future, with a cherry on top.

The weeks after I signed the letter of intent were a blur of checklists and caffeine, Atlanta style. There were calls with a lawyer Doris recommended, a final, bittersweet goodbye with my principal, and the surprisingly simple act of packing my life into six boxes. My month-to-month lease in Atlanta had been a safety net. Ending it felt less like cutting a cord and more like realizing there was nothing holding me in the first place. And now here I was.

I was on a stepladder, wrestling with a paint tarp in what would become the new stockroom, when my phone buzzed. It was Gloria from the bank.

"Brynn." Gloria's voice was warm and professional. "Just wanted to let you know the underwriters just gave the final sign-off. The loan is officially approved. The closing paperwork is ready when you are."

My knees went weak. I gripped the ladder, the phone pressed to my ear. "It's… it's really happening?"

"It's really happening," Gloria confirmed. "Congratulations. You're a business owner."

I hung up, my hand trembling, and slid down the ladder. I found Doris in the main shop, meticulously cleaning the nozzles on the old slush machine. I didn't know what to say, so the only thing that came out was a choked, "My loan was approved. Thank you." The two words seemed so inadequate.

She turned, wiping her hands on her apron, her expression softening when she saw my face. "For what? The loan was all you, kid. You earned it."

"For everything," I said, tears finally spilling over. "For trusting me. For seeing something in me I didn't see in myself."

Doris got a little misty-eyed, but she just pulled me into a rough, one-armed hug that smelled like sugar and Windex. "Don't get sappy on me. You still have to learn how to defrost the walk-in freezer without flooding the stockroom. Now, are you going to stand there crying, or are you going to help pick a new paint color?"

The Corner Scoop was mid-metamorphosis. Paint tarps were wadded in the corner, and at least three half-assembled freezer shelves half-blocked the path from back to front. The walls were a punchy seafoam that looked ridiculous on the paint chip but somehow perfect in the early light, especially with the salt-stained floors and the sun-faded *Homemade Since 1962* sign I'd convinced Doris not to touch. The whole shop vibrated with the kind of energy that comes from starting over. Every scuff and misaligned shelf was undeniable proof I wasn't utterly unambitious.

The first day I had keys to the place, I'd come in after midnight, lights off, just to run my hands along the Formica counter and convince myself it wasn't a dream. I could still feel the shiver of it. The way the hum of the old refrigeration units vibrated up through my palms. I could almost see Dean perched on one of the stools, arms crossed, making a deadpan joke about food safety or the tragic plight of the lactose intolerant. Sometimes I'd catch myself laughing at one of those ghostly jokes and had to pretend it was the radio.

It had been nearly a month since I'd last seen him. A month since he walked out of my bed, my life, and the entire state of Florida. He left nothing behind except a single button from his shirt, which I found on the floor and kept in my desk drawer because I am the world's softest mark. Just a few apologetic texts, but nothing that showed he was willing to stand up for what he wanted. Stand up for me.

I missed him so much it made my teeth hurt.

Maybe he was back in Atlanta, ruling his high-rise kingdom with the same ruthless efficiency he'd used to break my heart. Maybe he was already on to the next girl who thought she could melt him. The ache of missing him never really faded. It just disguised itself as other things. Most days, it wore the face of ambition. Sometimes it was hunger or the tightness in my chest when I wiped down the counter at closing and remembered his hands on my skin.

I shook myself and focused on organizing the sprinkles. Rainbow, chocolate, silver nonpareils for the wedding crowd, and those weird rock candy nuggets Doris bought on closeout. I would not be reordering those.

I caught my reflection in the curved surface of the cooler. My hair was twisted up in a bandana, my arms sticky with residue from the morning's lemon custard trial run. I looked like someone who belonged here. Maybe for the first time ever. So why did I feel like something was missing?

Doris stomped in from the rear of the store, red-faced but triumphant. "I'm gonna send out for breakfast sandwiches unless you plan on surviving on sugar today."

"Sugar is technically a food group," I said, but I smiled. "Bacon and egg, please."

She nodded and took her phone out, thumbs dancing across the screen. Then she looked up, all pretense of gruffness stripped away. "You're doing good, Brynn. This place is better for having you."

I blinked, surprised at the sting behind my eyes. "Thanks, Doris."

I returned to the sprinkles, but my hands were steadier now. Maybe that was all it took—one person believing in you, even when you couldn't quite believe in yourself. Maybe the leftover ache from Dean was just the price I had to pay for wanting something so badly it made me stupid with hope. I finished arranging the shelf and ran my fingers along the counter, right where I imagined Dean would rest his folded arms. The surface was cool and reassuring under my palm.

By noon, the shop was a pastel blur of cones, napkins, and toddler shrieks. The regulars trickled in, each with their predictable orders, and I found comfort in the monotony. Every vanilla swirl and double-scoop cookie dough was another brick in the foundation of my new life. It was working, mostly. It was healing, allegedly.

A stubborn canister of Mermaid Shimmer resisted my attempts to stack it, and I let out a sigh that echoed through the empty front. Doris, perched on a stool behind the register with a battered clipboard, looked up and raised her eyebrows. She set down the pen and propped her chin on her hands.

"Still thinking about that city boy, aren't you?" Her voice was as dry as plain oat bran.

I startled, nearly dropping the container. "Is it that obvious?"

"Honey, you've got the face of a woman who's either in love or has a particularly tenacious foot fungus." Doris's smile was gentle, her eyes sharper than ever. "You're lucky it's the first one."

I pretended to fuss over the shelf, but my ears burned. "I just—I can't believe I miss him this much. It wasn't even that long. We barely had time to know each other."

Doris snorted. "You're smarter than that, hon. Time doesn't mean a thing when it's right. A single minute can be enough to change your whole life."

I rolled a sprinkle jar between my palms, watching the glimmer through the plastic. "He said it was a vacation thing. A way to forget the real world."

She leaned forward, her voice softening. "And what do you think it was?"

"The first time I ever wanted to stay."

Doris watched me, nodding with a kind of pride that only comes from seeing someone finally get their head out of their own ass. "Maybe you should tell him that."

I shook my head. "What if he doesn't want to hear it?"

"Then he's not the man you need," Doris said simply. "And you're better off without him. But you told me he's texted you a few times. Maybe he's thinking the same thing about you right now."

I let her words sink in, the truth of them settling in my chest like a new kind of ache. Shaking my head, I wiped the counter with a clean rag.

Ten minutes later, the door opened, and my world narrowed to a single point of contact.

Dean stood just inside the threshold, suitcase in hand, his shirt rumpled and his hair wilder than I'd ever seen it. But his eyes locked on mine with an intensity that made my stomach turn inside out. For a second, I forgot to breathe.

Doris, sharp as ever, glanced between us, then slid off her stool and scurried to the back room.

Dean stepped forward, his jaw set and his gaze unblinking. I had no idea if I wanted to scream at him or wrap myself around him.

Probably both.

He looked like hell. Not in a post-breakup, can't-be-bothered sense, but like a man who'd been wrestling with himself for a month and finally surrendered. His eyes were bloodshot and wild, shirt untucked, duffel dangling from one hand. He strode forward and didn't stop until he was right in front of me, separated only by the glass display.

A buzzing sensation started in the soles of my feet and traveled up my legs, making the floor feel like it was vibrating. A full-body tremor rattled through me, equal parts stupefaction and a wild, impossible jolt of hope. I gripped the edge of the counter. "Dean… what?"

"I'm sorry," he said, his voice low and raw. "I know that's not enough, but it's where I have to start. I was a complete idiot. A coward, like you said." He ran a hand through his hair, the gesture ragged. "Your last text hit me like a knife in my gut, and you were right to send it. That's why I'm here. I'm done with texts. I had to see you, to tell you in person that I've missed you every single second since I walked out of that room."

I tried to find my anger, the sharp edge I'd been saving for this moment, but his words were like water on a flame, extinguishing it. All that was left was the raw, aching hurt. "You came all this way to tell me that?"

He smiled, lopsided, full of regret and hope in equal measure. Real. "I came here because I love you. I don't care if we were only together a few days. I realized I'd rather get it wrong a hundred times with you than pretend to get it right with anyone else."

All the oxygen left the room. Somewhere in back, Doris let out a sound that was definitely a sniff and maybe not a sob.

Did he just tell me he loves me?

My words tumbled out, like the last Jenga piece giving way. "I missed you. Every day, I missed you, and it was awful, and I hated myself for it, but—" My throat closed up, and I had to stop before I started ugly-crying in front of the freezer. I whipped my head back and forth. "You really hurt me."

He took a step closer and braced his hands on the counter. "Then let me fix it. Let me earn your forgiveness. By being here now. I will do whatever it takes."

I lifted my chin, a wall of self-preservation rising. "Dean, I can't. How do I know you won't take off again?"

"Because I've realized bolting out of that hotel room was the worst mistake I've ever made. And I won't let it happen again. You were right. I panicked because I realized I was falling for you, and I couldn't handle it. But that's over now."

He pulled his phone from his pocket and slid it across

the counter. It was open to a local real estate website, a listing for a storefront for sale on Main Street. I'd walked by it several times and admired the location.

"I've been looking at these listings ever since I left. Bookmarking every new one that came up. I've been picturing my own financial planning shingle hanging on Main Street, right under one of those ornate lampposts with the flower baskets I used to think were so stupid. But they're not. I was stupid."

My lungs were about to burst, and I slowly exhaled a month of misery. A fresh breath of hope took its place.

"I spent the last three years building a life I thought I wanted," he continued, his eyes laser-focused on mine. "The high-rise, the title, the six-figure salary… it was all a reaction to being hurt. It was a shield. But in those few days with you, I felt more real than I ever have in my life. And it scared me so badly that I panicked. I ran."

I could read the truth of his words in his eyes, in the exhausted lines around his mouth. New warmth filled my chest. I nodded at him as I wrapped my arms around myself, holding on. "Go on."

"I'm still scared, but not about getting close." His voice dropped, becoming more intense. "I'm scared of living a life without you in it. I don't want Atlanta. I want this right here. I want the flower baskets, the gossip, and the ice cream. I want you."

He reached across the counter and entwined his fingers with mine. "Please forgive me. Let me try. I will show up for you every single day. Forever, if you'll let me."

Every instinct I had honed screamed at me to protect myself, to remember the emptiness of that hotel room. But what I saw in his eyes wasn't just regret. It was resolve. He hadn't returned with pretty words—he had returned with a plan. He had quit his job, found a new place to build a life, and taken a risk that was a thousand times bigger than the one I took signing a loan document.

I squeezed his hand back. "You are a persuasive man. A little infuriating too."

A flicker of a smile touched his lips. "I know. I'm working on it."

"Your timing is terrible."

"Also working on it."

I looked at him, at the genuine, desperate hope in his eyes, and the last of my defenses crumbled. A smile raised my lips that was only a little shaky. "You really quit your job?"

He nodded, his expression dead serious. "Two-week notice. It was the best feeling of my life. I can be here permanently within a few weeks."

I couldn't help it. I started laughing, a messy, weird sound of disbelief and relief. Because that's what happened when the man who broke your heart showed up and proved he was willing to shatter his entire world just for a chance to help you build yours.

The counter between us felt less like a workspace and more like a barrier. I didn't think, just moved. I planted my hands on the cool granite, hoisted myself up, and swung over, landing in front of him with a slightly unsteady thud. His eyes widened, and a rough, incredulous laugh broke from his chest, full of shock and something that looked a lot like hope.

"Brynn—" he started, but I didn't let him finish.

I launched myself into his arms, wrapping my legs around his waist and my arms around his neck, and kissed him. I kissed him with all the hurt, hope, and lonely weeks I had just endured. It was a hard, wet, desperate kiss, and he met it with a ferocity that matched my own. His hands gripped my butt, holding me tightly as if he were afraid I might disappear.

When we finally broke apart, both of us were breathless and smiling like fools.

"So does this mean I get a second chance?"

"Yeah, you big jerk." I wiped my nose and tried to scowl, but I was smiling too hard. "Because I love you too. Should we celebrate with ice cream?"

As he set me back on my feet, his grin broadened. "How about I take my girlfriend out on an official date? I hear there's a great resort brewpub on the western edge of the island that makes the best beer in the Lower Keys. Sounds like a great place for a new start."

"It is. I can vouch for that."

And he kissed me again. Doris was openly sniffling from the back room, not even pretending not to watch. Our lips melded to each other's, and it was even sweeter than ice cream.

I'd spent most of my life waiting for something to happen. For someone to choose me, for the world to make sense, for happiness to finally stick. But maybe happiness wasn't about waiting at all.

Maybe it was about choosing to be brave, even when it scared you.

Especially when it scared you.

Chapter Ten

DEAN

IF I HAD WRITTEN a playbook for the world's most backward, inefficient, and emotionally chaotic path to a first date, it wouldn't have matched what happened between Brynn and me. Yet this playbook was perfect. It started with a lie at a wedding mixer, escalated to a public kiss, and ended right back where the whole charade began.

Tropical Hops was the same cozy craft brewery on a breezy island, with the cheery turquoise walls I always mocked but secretly liked, and that battered longboard mounted above the taps like it was the Ark of the Covenant. Once again, Braden Coleridge was tending bar. The place was slow this afternoon, just a couple of retirees at the far end and a sunburned couple making out like they'd invented kissing.

Braden spotted us, grinned, and headed our way. "Hey, you two look familiar. Brynn, definitely. Weren't you at the same wedding?" he asked me. After a very abbreviated explanation that she was a new Dove Key resident and I would be soon, he lit up. "In that case, first round's on the house. Unless you want something top shelf, in which case, I'll pretend I don't know you."

"We'll take one of your IPAs," I said with a grin. "Surprise us."

"You got it," Braden said, then turned to Brynn as he pulled the tap. "You keeping him out of trouble?"

"No," she deadpanned. "But I'm documenting every moment for the trial."

He laughed and indicated he'd bring our beers to us.

After we settled into a private booth, I couldn't stop looking at her. The lighting was criminally flattering, and she'd let her hair down, signaling we were done pretending to be responsible. Even her smile was looser.

Braden arrived, setting down two frosty pint glasses with a flourish. "Tidal Hops IPA. My flagship beer. Let me officially welcome you to Dove Key, Brynn. And Dean"—he clapped me on the shoulder—"congratulations on discovering life in the slow lane."

"Sounds like a great toast to drink to." I raised my glass. The IPA was all citrus and pine, cold enough to bite. For a while, we sat, soaking in the lazy drift of conversation from the bar, where Braden had returned and was chatting with a regular.

Brynn's eyes scanned the pub, a smile spreading across her face. "I can't believe we're here again. It still doesn't feel real. Doris is giving me three months to learn the ropes before I'm fully on my own."

"You'll be fine. You might even be overqualified."

Brynn grinned, then her expression turned serious. "I'm scared I'll fail. That it'll go south like all the other times I've tried something for myself and crashed."

I set down my beer. "That's not how I see you at all."

She raised an eyebrow, as if daring me to say more.

"You're the opposite of a quitter," I told her. "Even when some idiot like me tells you it doesn't matter, you stick to your guns."

She looked away, blinking quickly. "What if it isn't enough?"

"Then I'll catch you. And if I fail as a small-town financial advisor, you can throw ice cream at me until I'm unrecognizable."

Brynn laughed, then lifted her pint for a toast. "To new beginnings."

"And to hoping we don't suck at them."

We clinked glasses again. This time, it felt like a promise.

Then the front door clattered open, and in walked Austin and Eli Coleridge, looking like they'd just rolled out of a beer commercial. Austin's shirt was clean but somehow already untucked, and Eli wore a rash guard and board shorts, his hair a sandstorm of cowlicks. They headed Braden's way and the three heads converged. Then surprise flitted over Eli's and Austin's faces.

They beelined for our booth, Eli in the lead, a massive grin spreading across his face.

"Mercer!" he boomed, sliding into the booth next to me with enough force to rock the whole table. "Braden just gave us the rundown. A fake relationship that turned real? That is the most ridiculously romantic thing I've ever heard. I'm impressed. I didn't think you had it in you."

Austin slipped in next to Brynn. He nodded at her, then me, with a flicker of something like approval in his cautious gray eyes. "So you're sticking around, huh?"

"That's the plan." A warmth spread through my chest that had nothing to do with the IPA. "Assuming the town will have me."

"Oh, we'll have you," Eli declared, clapping me on the

shoulder. "We're always looking for new talent for the annual conch-shell-blowing contest. You look like you've got strong lungs." He waggled his eyebrows at Brynn, who couldn't hide her smile. "So, when's the grand opening of the new Scoop?"

"We're having a low-key opening next week," Brynn said. "If I survive Doris's training boot camp."

Austin pointed a finger at me, a hint of a smile raising his lips. "If you're gonna stick around, you'll need to learn how to handle a rod. It's embarrassing otherwise. I'll take you out sometime. Show you the basics, so you have a shot at keeping up with Brynn."

I tried to laugh it off, but the offer felt damn good. Like a formal welcome ceremony for a local. "Thanks. I'd love that."

Eli launched into a wild story, mostly directed at Austin, about a grouper that nearly capsized their cousin's boat. Austin just rolled his eyes.

Brynn leaned close and whispered, "See? I told you they're all softies."

I looked at the battered longboard, the turquoise walls, the people who'd already decided I was one of their own.

And I felt it, for the first time. Belonging.

The second round went down smoother than the first. Eventually, the Coleridge brothers moved on to an impromptu darts tournament, and Brynn and I were alone again.

"So, where are you staying?" I asked, the practical question rising to the surface.

"I'm in a little rental flat for now. Doris is still in the apartment above the Corner Scoop. She's got to pack up a lifetime of stuff before she moves in with her sister, so I told her to take her time." She smiled a little shyly. "It's a mess, but it's mine for now. What are your plans?"

"I'll head back to Atlanta tomorrow. I gave two weeks' notice, so I'll need that time to wrap up my projects. Then probably another week to pack up my life and get out of my lease."

Her smile faltered for a second. "You'll be gone three weeks?"

"No longer," I promised, reaching across the table to take her hand. "You don't need to worry about me staying there. I'll be making some calls starting tomorrow. That listing I showed you in the ice cream shop—a space on Main Street a couple of blocks from the Scoop—really caught my eye."

"Yeah?" she asked, her eyes lighting up.

I grinned. "Yeah. I'm going to put an offer on it ASAP. It's not huge, but it's got great visibility. And a one-bedroom apartment right above it, so both our living situations could be set right out of the gate."

Brynn's mouth formed a perfect *O*, then broke into a wide, beautiful smile. "You're kidding."

"Nope," I said, a wave of pride rising. "As soon as I saw it, I had a feeling that was the one. I've gotten better at recognizing that over the last month."

Brynn's smile faltered as she twisted a napkin. "Do you ever worry that we're just setting ourselves up to fail? That this is all too much, too fast?"

"Maybe," I admitted. "But I'd rather try and fail than chicken out before the starting gun."

"Me too." She squeezed my hand, her eyes shining. "New homes for each of us. We could fix them both up together."

"I'd offer to help, but I nearly lost a finger assembling IKEA shelves last year."

"Maybe not such a great idea," she said with a teasing laugh. "But I like the idea of you trying."

The future, which had been a formless void just a few days ago, was now a blueprint. A complicated, wonderful blueprint we could build together.

When we left, the late sun was a melted orange over the sea, turning the water to copper. Brynn looped her arm through mine as we navigated the sidewalk. We strolled slowly, in no hurry, the evening breeze thick with salt and possibility.

"Wanna come up?" Brynn asked, nodding to the row of brightly painted townhouses up the next block. "You can see my hand-me-down sofa. It's a real work of art."

"Lead the way," I said. "I need to see what I'm up against."

The short walk was full of lazy conversation—plans for porch furniture, which sports teams we'd support if forced at gunpoint, where to get the best Cuban sandwich within fifty miles.

We reached her door. Brynn unlocked it and gestured for me to step inside. The place was barely furnished, with a few cardboard boxes by the entryway and a navy-blue sofa that looked like it had survived several hurricanes. The kitchen was clean and relatively updated. On the counter sat a single mug, bright yellow, with *TEACHERS ARE MAGIC* in blue glitter.

"Make yourself at home," Brynn said, kicking off her shoes.

The space was unassuming, but it already radiated her personality—practical, a little messy, endlessly hopeful.

"I like it," I said.

"You don't have to pretend. The sofa's a disaster and the air conditioning sounds like it's experiencing a painful death."

I shrugged one shoulder. "Feels more like home than anywhere I've lived in years."

She went quiet, eyes shining. "Just wait a few months when we're settled in, huh?"

We stood there for a moment, neither of us moving, the gravity between us suddenly too strong to ignore. She stepped forward and wrapped her arms around my waist, resting her cheek against my chest. I hugged her back, feeling her heartbeat match mine.

"Remember when I said this place wasn't real life?" I murmured into her hair. "I couldn't have been more wrong. This is the only thing that's ever felt real."

She squeezed tighter. "It always has been for me. I'm just glad you see it too."

She pulled back just enough to look up at me, her hands finding the line of my jaw, the heat of her palms seeping through my skin. I let myself sink into it, the slow burn of her mouth as she kissed me, the thrum of desire starting low and spreading outward until it was the only thing I could feel.

When she finally broke the kiss, she was breathless. "So, you've seen the lovely kitchen and living room. Want a tour of the bedroom?"

My voice was a low rasp. "Is that where the real magic happens?"

"Only one way to find out," she murmured, taking my hand and leading me down the short hallway.

We didn't let go of each other, stumbling into the room in a jumble of limbs and mouths. The bedroom was as simple and hopeful as the rest of the apartment—a queen bed with a white comforter, a stack of books on the floor, and moonlight spilling through the open window.

The air was thick with unspoken promises. This time was different. Not the frantic collision of two people at the end of a wedding. This was a beginning.

I reached for the hem of her shirt, my movements slow

and deliberate. She watched me as I drew the fabric up and over her head, letting it fall to the floor. I undressed her with reverence, unhooking her bra, unbuttoning her shorts, my fingers tracing the lines of her body as if I were memorizing a map.

When she was bare and standing in a pool of moonlight, I studied her for a moment, my chest tight with an emotion too big to name. She didn't try to cover herself. She held my gaze, offering a vulnerability I was desperate to protect.

She reached for the buttons on my shirt, her hands trembling slightly as she worked them free. We remained silent, every touch a question and an answer, until there was nothing between us but the cool night air and the heavy weight of everything we'd almost lost.

I lifted her into my arms and carried her the last few feet to the bed, letting her fall back onto the soft comforter. As she moved beneath the covers, I followed her down, settling between her legs, her body parting for me in a silent, perfect invitation.

Her skin was electric. I could feel her tense and relax, her breath catching each time my hand moved. I palmed the curve of her ass, pulled her tight against me, and she arched in response, her mouth finding my neck.

I took my time. I kissed her jaw, the hollow behind her ear, the delicate ridge of her collarbone. I slid my hand between her thighs, feeling the damp heat.

"Oh, yes," she breathed.

I circled my fingers, slow at first, watching her face for every twitch and shiver. She closed her eyes, biting her lip, her thighs trembling as I worked her higher. I added a finger, and her whole body jerked in response.

"Dean—" she gasped.

I didn't let up. I kissed her again, deep and claiming.

"Let go for me," I whispered against her lips.

She did. She climaxed with a shudder, back arched, nails digging into my shoulders. I watched her ride it out, her face slack with pleasure. I stroked her through the aftershocks, kissing her forehead, her cheeks, her lips.

When she could speak again, she gave me a cocky smile. "You were always good at showing off." She reached for me, bracing my hips with both hands. "Your turn."

I shook my head. "No."

She gave me a look—half challenge, half invitation. "You're going to make me beg?"

"There's an idea," I said with a grin. "Put that one in the memory file."

Instead, I grabbed my wallet out of my shorts and rolled on the condom. As I settled above her, she surprised me by rolling me onto my back and climbing astride me, her hair falling around her face like a curtain. She took my shaft in her hand, stroking it slowly, her eyes locked on mine. When she lined herself up and sank down, it was torture—hot, tight, perfect.

I GROANED, gripping her hips, trying to hold on as she started to ride me. She moved slowly at first, grinding down, her eyes closed, a soft sigh escaping her lips as she tested the rhythm. I let her take the lead, my hands roaming from the curve of her waist to the smooth skin of her back, every part of me content to just follow.

When she picked up the pace, the sight of her completely unraveled me. She threw her head back, her long hair cascading down her back, the muscles in her throat defined in the moonlight from the window. She was completely lost in the moment, in the pleasure, utterly and beautifully unguarded.

All the noise in my head—the projections, the years of self-imposed rules—it all just stopped. There was only her and pure, unfiltered honesty. This was the real life I'd run from. Not a liability to be managed, but a truth to be lived. And it was the most captivating thing I had ever witnessed.

She leaned down then, her hair tenting around us, her mouth at my ear. "You're mine, and don't forget it."

The words, so fierce and possessive, shot through me. "Always."

I thrust up, hard, and she cried out, her body shuddering. I grabbed her ass, holding her in place as I took her deeper, harder.

"Brynn," I groaned, "I'm so close…"

She covered my mouth with hers, kissing me through it, her body squeezing me so tight I almost saw stars. I climaxed inside her, hips jerking, hands clutching her as if I could fuse us together. She whimpered, her whole body shaking in my arms.

We collapsed in a heap, her head on my chest, my arms around her. For a long time, there was only the sound of our breathing.

I traced lazy circles on her back. "This," I said, my voice husky, "right here is what I was so afraid of."

She propped herself up on an elbow, her expression soft and questioning. "Being with me?"

"Not just that. Feeling this real. I didn't think I could handle it." I smiled, burying my face in her hair. "Turns out I can't live without it."

A soft, deep breath escaped her, and she lowered her head back to my chest, her cheek warm against my skin. Her hand came up to rest over my heart, as if she could feel the truth of the words beating there.

We lay in the quiet, the moonlight painting silver stripes across the rumpled sheets. The promise of morning and a thousand new beginnings waited just outside the door. There were still moves to be made, businesses to build, and a lifetime of arguments over whose turn it was to take out the trash. It was weird and complicated and scary.

And for the first time, I knew I was exactly where I was supposed to be.

When I dreamed, it was of salt and sunlight, and the taste of her laughter on my tongue.

Epilogue

BRYNN

Not so long ago, I'd have bet every dollar in my bank account that the phrase *dream come true* was reserved for lottery winners, new parents, and people who collected inspirational magnets. But as I stood behind the polished quartz counter of The Corner Scoop's Grand Re-Opening, surveying a sea of happy, sunburned faces, I realized I'd become that cliché—the girl with the happy ending.

The shop was alive, a joyful collision of sound and sugar. The walls, freshly painted a pale robin's-egg blue, glowed in the afternoon sun. Above the counter, a chalkboard menu listed every flavor I'd ever dared to create, written in my own loopy, imperfect handwriting—a declaration of independence in chalk dust. The far wall showcased local artists: ocean photography, driftwood sculptures, and an impressionist portrait of a manatee that looked suspiciously like Eli Coleridge if you squinted. The place was packed, a line snaking out the door and onto the sidewalk. The bell over the door chimed so often I'd started hearing it in my sleep, a constant punctuation mark in my new life.

Best of all, I wasn't drowning. I wasn't even treading water. I was swimming, head above the surface, arms strong and steady.

I handed off a waffle cone piled high with Sandbar Cookie Crunch and braced myself on the counter, pausing for the first time all afternoon. For a beat, I let myself remember who I'd been that first day in Dove Key—a girl terrified she'd peaked at *utterly unambitious*, a woman so scared of even trying she'd almost let her ex-boyfriend's bitter words become her truth. Now I was someone who'd gutted a small business and rebuilt it from the studs up, who was recognized at the bank, and who had a favorite place to watch the sunrise with the man I loved. The realization hit with a force that made my eyes sting.

The Coleridge siblings had taken over a corner of the shop, turning it into their personal headquarters. Harper was perched at a high-top, her manager's eye instinctively critiquing my new employee Sydney's attempt at a rainbow sprinkle gradient, though a smile played on her lips. She caught my eye and tipped me a wink. Braden was telling a story with wild hand gestures to a table of off-duty marina workers, his laughter booming over the din. And Eli, true to form, had already charmed his way behind the counter, shamelessly quality-checking samples with the gusto of a child left alone in a candy store. He'd just slung an arm around my shoulder, declaring to the room at large that I was "the best damn ice cream maker in three counties."

That was when I spotted Dean, leaning in the doorway, hands in the pockets of his slacks, an expression I'd learned to read as fondly exasperated. He was tan, his hair a little longer and messier than it used to be, and he wore a relaxed, open smile I'd once believed existed only in vacation commercials. He looked gorgeous. He looked happy.

He navigated the crowd, sidestepping a gaggle of grade-schoolers with the ease of someone who now considered this his natural habitat. He paused at the counter, scanning the chaos before settling on me. "You know, for a Grand Re-Opening, this feels more like a city-wide block party. Did you forget to charge people?"

I grinned, my cheeks aching from smiling all day. "You have Doris to thank for the turnout. She may have moved to be closer to her grandkids, but she still runs this town by text. I think she threatened the entire Rotary Club with eternal damnation if they didn't show up."

"Of course she did," he said, taking my hand in a quick, private squeeze. I felt it down to my toes. He leaned closer. "So, is it finally ready?"

My heart did a little flip. "It's ready. I was waiting for the official taste tester to arrive."

"I take my duties very seriously."

I ducked into the back freezer and returned with a small paper cup of a flavor we hadn't put on the menu yet, a secret I'd been perfecting with Sydney for weeks. It was a gorgeous swirl of deep, glossy chocolate threaded with bright ribbons of gold. I passed it to him.

"Sydney and I finally nailed the salt content in the caramel," I said, trying to sound casual. "I'm calling it Sunset Charade Swirl."

I watched Dean's face as he took the first bite. The chocolate was dark, bordering on bitter, but the caramel—shockingly rich and just salty enough—smoothed out every edge. It was a little sharp, a little sweet, and a lot more complicated than it looked.

It was us.

He closed his eyes for a moment, savoring it. When he opened them, his forehead had gone slack. "Brynn, this is absolutely perfect. And not just for us."

Finally, the crowd began to thin. Braden came over. "Gotta run, guys. Time to make the beer. Place looks amazing, Brynn. Seriously. From one business owner to another, you've done great work here." Pride filled me at his praise. After exchanging nods, he traipsed out the door.

Eli approached and clapped Dean on the back. He hooked an arm over my shoulder and pointed to Braden's retreating form. "Hey, there are going to be two-for-ones at Tidal Hops tonight. You guys should come by."

My heart leaped. I looked at Dean, and he was smiling, already knowing what I was thinking.

"Sounds great," he said, his voice easy. "Perfect place to catch the sunset."

He met my eyes, and the promise of the evening to come showed in their depths. As the Coleridge brothers headed out, Dean slipped his hand into the pocket of his pants, a subtle gesture I almost missed. I couldn't think of a better way to end the perfect day.

Several hours later, the buzz of Tidal Hops faded behind us. It was replaced by the gentle lap of water as Dean led me to the long wooden pier with its weathered planks. As much as I loved my own slice of Dove Key, Sunset Siesta Resort was the place where I'd first connected with him, a handsome co-wedding attendant trapped in a conversation. Though Dean was a local now, this was where our ridiculous, wonderful charade had begun. Every step was charged with memories of our first night, the solidness of his hand in mine, the ghost of a kiss that had changed everything.

We walked past the quiet dive shop to the end of the dock. We stopped, leaning against the railing as the sun melted into the Gulf. The sky flared, a riot of impossible orange and hot pink, the colors so intense it almost hurt to look.

Dean turned to face me, his eyes reflecting the fiery sky. "I used to think sunsets like this were a cliché. Just a predictable, overly sentimental ending to the day. A distraction from real life."

I nudged him with my shoulder. "And now, O Cynical One?"

He shook his head, a wry smile on his lips. "Now I know my life in Atlanta was the fantasy. An emptiness I built out of fear." He took both of my hands in his, his grip warm and steady. "The moments I spent with you on this pier, at this resort, even when we were pretending, were the first time in years I felt like myself. You, this town, this living, sunburned heartbeat of a place... This is the real life I want."

My heart did a slow, squeezing flip in my chest.

The sun lit the pier ablaze in twenty shades of gold. "I spent my entire career analyzing risk," he continued. "And I know, with absolute certainty, that the biggest risk of my life would be letting another day go by without you in it."

Letting go of my hands, he reached into his pocket and pulled out a small, dark velvet box. He dropped to one knee on the weathered wood of the pier and opened it. The ring inside caught the last of the sun, refracting it into a small, defiant miracle. A starburst exploding with light that caused goosebumps to pebble the skin of my arms.

"Brynn," he said, his voice clear and steady, "you are

the bravest, most real, most beautiful person I've ever known. Will you marry me and make my life real forever?"

The world went silent, except for the wild, joyful beating of my heart. I stared at him—at his face, his hope, the risk he'd taken for me. I'd never been surer of anything in my life.

A laugh, bright and tear-soaked, bubbled out of me. "Are you kidding me? Hell yes, Mercer! Absolutely, one thousand times yes."

Laughing, he rushed out a breath and surged to his feet. He slid the ring onto my finger, and I pulled him into a kiss that tasted like sugar, home, and forever.

He held me close, his arms a solid weight around my shoulders, and we stood together as the last sliver of sun disappeared below the horizon. The island was ours, plus our future was wide open. And nothing about it was fake.

THANK you for reading SUNSET CHARADE! If you enjoyed the book, it would mean the world to me if you left a short review on Amazon, Goodreads, or Bookbub. Reviews are so important to independent authors to help other readers discover books. I appreciate your support!

Keep reading to see what comes next…

Second Epilogue

ELI

The morning dive charter had just left. From where I stood behind the counter of Sunset Siesta's dive shop, *Sunset Diver* motored away from the pier, its wake a temporary scar on the placid turquoise water. Andrea was leading the group, her curly brown ponytail whipping in the breeze, her confidence obvious even from here. The shop was quiet now, filled only with the hum of spinning fans and the sharp, clean scent of neoprene I'd come to associate with home.

Leaning back, I scanned my domain. The aquamarine walls were covered in a collection of underwater photos I'd taken over the years, vibrant fish staring out like curious neighbors. Racks of wetsuits and BCDs stood like a silent, loyal army, ready for the next adventure. This was my sanctuary, my kingdom. I liked to think I was pretty good at teaching scuba diving safely while making the whole damn thing fun too.

Then I barked a laugh. Yeah, out loud. I was going to need some mental bleach strong enough to scrub away the image of Dean Mercer and Brynn Vance being so disgustingly cute at my brother's brewpub last night. Seriously, the two of them were a hazard. All those soft, secret smiles and the way he looked at her like she was the only person on the planet. I was happy for them, though. Brynn had been coming here since she was a teenager. Back then, she was a quiet, watchful kid with a lost look in her eyes. It had been cool to see the island work its magic on her over the years, to watch her come back and finally claim her place here.

She was one of us now.

And Dean… Hell, the guy had turned out to be surprisingly decent once you got past the city-boy armor. Seeing them together was enough to make a commitment-phobe like me break out in a cold sweat. Their brand of happy-ever-after was a foreign language to me. My relationships were simple, easy, and came with a clear expiration date.

My gaze drifted back to the dive boat, now a white speck on the horizon. Andrea was a rock. She'd been with us for two years, never missing a beat, her passion for the ocean almost rivaling my own. She showed up early, stayed late, and handled nervous divers with calm patience. She'd more than earned a little something extra.

The impulsive idea flashed. I was going to give her a raise. Maybe not a huge one, but something to show her she was doing good work. The thought sent a surge of satisfaction through me. Hell, it felt good to be the fun boss who could make things happen.

Then reality, as it so often did, crashed the party. My good mood deflated like a cheap pool float. Any decision that involved money—even a single, unauthorized roll of duct tape—had to get past the financial fortress of Sunset Siesta.

It had to go through *her*.

My nemesis. The Evil Queen of Accounting. Julianne Verne.

I could picture her now, sitting in her sterile, silent office, her almost-black hair pulled back in a bun so tight it probably gave her a headache. She likely had line items in the resort's budget specifically for Crushing Dreams and Denying Reasonable Requests. The woman could suck the fun out of a free-for-all at a beach party.

A sigh escaped me, then turned into a groan. This was going to be a battle. She'd pull out spreadsheets, cite quarterly projections, and hit me with a barrage of soul-crushing buzzwords like *fiscal responsibility* and *budgetary constraints*. I dreaded the confrontation, the inevitable clash of my carefree philosophy against her cold, hard logic.

But another part, a smaller, more stubborn part I didn't like to acknowledge, experienced a familiar thrill—a flash of anticipation. Asking for a raise was a long shot, and asking for an off-cycle raise was like asking a shark to go vegan. But hey, I was never one to back away from a challenge.

"Right," I drawled, pushing off the counter. Time to slay the dragon. Or at least try not to get incinerated.

The resort's main lobby building was always blissfully cooler than the rest of the world, the air-conditioned hush a contrast to the lively, sun-drenched noise outside. I walked down the hall, my flip-flops making a happy slapping sound against the polished tile. I passed Harper's office before stopping at the last door on the right.

Her door.

Julianne's office was exactly what you'd expect. A shrine to order. The scent of coconut air freshener fought a losing battle against the sterile smell of printer ink and overwhelming responsibility. Her desk was a vast, empty landscape of polished wood, with a keyboard, an ancient monitor, and a single, sad-looking cactus as its only inhabitants. Even the books on her shelf looked like they were standing at attention, arranged with military precision. It was the complete opposite of my comfortable, cluttered dive shop.

I put on my game face, the one that had charmed tourists out of their diving nerves and talked customs agents out of searching my boat. I sauntered in, not waiting for an invitation, and perched on the corner of her imposing desk. Yep, I was right. Her bun looked tight enough to bounce quarters off. Too bad I didn't have any with me.

She didn't look up. Her focus was absolute on the glowing spreadsheet on her screen. Her fingers flew across the keyboard with a speed that was both impressive and a little terrifying.

"Morning, Julianne," I said, my voice dripping with the easy charm I was laying on thick. "Don't let me interrupt your very important counting."

That got her. Her fingers stilled, and she slowly lifted her head. Her green eyes, sharp as sea glass, pinned me with a look that could freeze saltwater. She wore her work uniform of a crisp, white button-down shirt and a severe navy-blue skirt.

"Coleridge," she said, her voice as starched as her collar. "To what do I owe this intrusion? Did you get lost on your way to the beach?"

"Funny. No, I'm here on official business." I leaned forward, giving her my most earnest look. "I wanted to talk to you about Andrea. She's a rock star divemaster, going above and beyond. I've decided she's earned an extra raise, and I'm here to make it happen." I leaned back, crossing my arms with a magnanimous air. I was the good guy, the benevolent boss. How could she say no?

"That's very thoughtful, Eli," she said, swiveling her chair to face me fully, her expression unchanging. "However, annual performance reviews and raises were completed two months ago. There is no room in the current quarter's budget for an ad-hoc salary increase."

Her response was so immediate and perfectly recited that I had to wonder if she had a pre-recorded message for this exact scenario.

"Come on, Julianne," I pressed, hopping off the desk to pace in front of it. It was time for Plan B: Appeal to Her Humanity (Good Luck). "We're not talking about numbers on a page. We're talking about morale. Happy staff, happy guests. It's a win-win."

"My job is to ensure the resort remains solvent, Coleridge, not to play fairy godmother with payroll." She tapped a manicured finger on a stack of reports. "And according to these numbers, our solvency is… tenuous. A discretionary raise is simply not a responsible use of our limited resources."

I stopped pacing and leaned my hands on the back of the visitor's chair, fixing her with a look I hoped conveyed passionate reason. "You're all about the long game, right? Investing? This is an investment in our most valuable asset: our people. Andrea is a key part of the dive operation's success. We need to show her she's valued."

"I know her very well, and I like her too. But she's valued every two weeks when her direct deposit hits her bank account," she retorted, her voice dry as sand. "An out-of-cycle raise sets a dangerous precedent, Eli. If we do it for Andrea, what's to stop every other employee from lining up outside my door demanding the same?"

This woman was an impenetrable fortress of logic. "Because what Andrea does is a hell of a lot harder—and more dangerous—than pouring drinks or staring at a screen in a nice, air-conditioned office. And because they'd have to get through you, and let's be honest, your glare is more effective than a moat full of sharks."

For the first time, a flicker of something other than icy professionalism crossed her face. Was that amusement? It was gone before I could be sure. "While I appreciate the backhanded compliment, my glare isn't a recognized line item in our budget. The answer is no."

The energy in the room was almost physical, a current of antagonism that, if I was being honest, was more invigorating than a shot of espresso. I loved rattling her cage, loved seeing the cracks appear in her polished armor. I was losing, badly, but I'd be damned if I was going down without a fight. "You're a boat anchor, Julianne. You just drag everything right down to the bottom." I took a breath. She was starting to get to me, dammit.

"I'm fiscally responsible," she countered, her voice infuriatingly calm. "Perhaps if you spent more time working on your payroll and less time working on your tan, you'd understand the position we're in."

"Ouch," I said, pressing a hand to my heart. "And here I thought we were bonding."

"Oh, no. Never."

Julianne swiveled in her ergonomic chair. She turned to a low, battleship-gray filing cabinet behind her, the very picture of efficient dismissal. The movement was crisp and meant to signal that our conversation was over.

It also made her skirt ride up.

Just a few inches. But it was enough. My eyes dropped, a purely instinctual reaction I couldn't have stopped if I'd tried. A long, graceful line of creamy skin was revealed from her knee up her thigh. It was a perfect leg—toned, elegant, ending in a curve that my brain registered with the force of a lightning strike. Then she shifted again, and the hem of her skirt fell back into place, hiding the evidence.

Whoa.

My mouth went dry. *Okay. Did not see that coming.*

Since when did the Evil Queen have legs like *that?* A jolt of pure, inconvenient heat shot through me, and it pissed me off. I snapped my gaze back up to her face, a flush creeping up my neck. She was pulling a file from the drawer, completely oblivious. Thank God.

Realizing I had lost this round, my charm and arguments useless against her castle of fiscal prudence, my good humor evaporated. I threw my hands up in a gesture of defeat. She turned back around, the file in her hand, her expression once again cool and impassive.

"Was there anything else?" she asked, her tone polished and utterly final.

I glared at her, at the neat bun, the sensible blouse, the stupidly sexy leg.

"Not today, Julianne," I snarled. "But this isn't over."

I stalked out of her office, the scent of her coconut air freshener and my own frustration mocking me. Fine. I didn't care if she had the legs of a supermodel or the mind of a damn calculator. If she wanted a war over a damn budget, I'd bring the heat.

***

Continue your visit to Sunset Siesta by diving into Book 1 of the series,

BETTER THAN NEVER: A Small Town Enemies to Lovers Romance
Sunset Siesta Series

She's my workplace enemy—now my student, and way too tempting. The ocean's deep, but this forbidden trouble runs deeper.

Eli:

In our small town of Dove Key, Julianne Verne and I are known for one thing. We clash spectacularly over every aspect of my family's resort where we both work. She's the meticulously organized accountant thriving on order, while I'm the laid-back dive instructor thriving on anything but. We're fire and ice in the Florida Keys, enemies and opposites in every way.

But now, I'm her unwilling scuba instructor for a wild wedding stunt. The close proximity is doing dangerous things to our long-standing animosity. Suddenly, her knife-sharp wit sounds more like playful banter. Our intense glares are looking a lot like smoldering glances. Then we combust in a beach shack.

This attraction is a forbidden complication I don't need. Especially with Mom's no-workplace-romances rule threatening to capsize everything. But I'm starting to think this captivating, infuriating woman might be the one adventure I can't resist.

Read BETTER THAN NEVER, book one of the interconnected small-town Sunset Siesta series, and discover why sometimes the best adventures begin with your worst enemy.

BETTER THAN NEVER: A Small Town Enemies to Lovers Romance
Sunset Siesta Series

Also by Erin Brockus

SUNSET SIESTA SERIES:

Sunset Charade: A Sunset Siesta Novella

*Available free to subscribers

Better than Never: A Small Town Enemies to Lovers Romance

Better than Home: Book 2 coming early 2026!

CALYPSO KEY SERIES:

MAIN NOVELS:

Visions of You: A Small Town Single Dad Romance

Because of You: A Small Town Fake Relationship Romance

Memories of You: A Small Town Second Chance Romance

Shades of You: A Small Town Forbidden Romance

Associated Short Stories and Novellas:

Traces of You: A Small Town Rivals to Lovers Romance*

* Subscriber exclusive

ISLAND ESCAPES SERIES:

In Too Deep: A Second Chance Romance

Beached in Bali: A Friends to Lovers Romance

Betting on Paradise: A Fake Relationship Billionaire Romance

Clock Strikes Paradise: Coming mid-2025!

HALF MOON BAY SERIES:

Dive into steamy small-town romance, where passion meets paradise!

Award-winning author Erin Brockus writes steamy small town romances that transport readers to exotic, tropical destinations, and provide a perfect beachy getaway from everyday life. Her mature, relatable characters are impossible not to root for, and she weaves breezy romantic adventure into her stories, emphasizing scuba diving and the ocean.

Drawing on her twin passions for diving and travel, Erin infuses her characters and narratives with a sense of excitement and passion. Her idea of the perfect day involves sipping a cocktail on the beach after exploring the ocean depths.

Erin lives in Washington wine country with her husband, who is also a scuba instructor. She is currently hard at work on her next island adventure. When she's not writing, she enjoys running, mountain biking, or enjoying a good book with a cup of coffee.